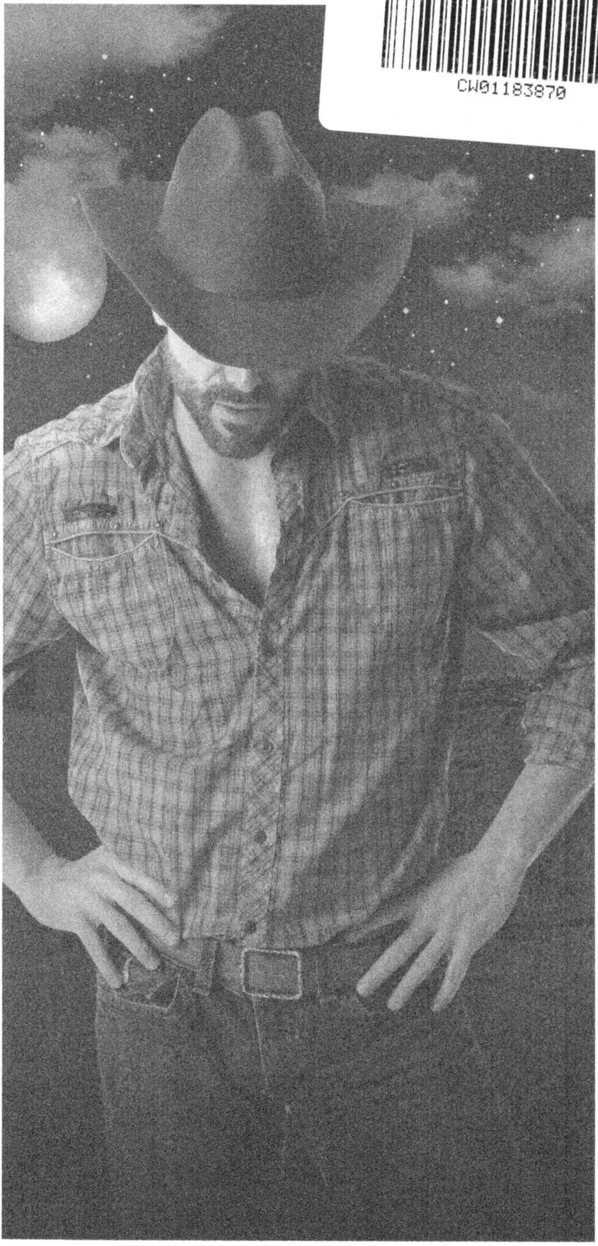

CHARMING A BIG BAD TEXAN

Copyright © 2022 by Katie Lane

All rights reserved. Except for use in any review, the reproduction or utilization of this work in whole or in part in any form by any electronic, mechanical or other means, now known or hereinafter invented, including xerography, photocopying and recording, or in any information storage or retrieval system, is forbidden without the written permission of the publisher.

This book is a work of fiction. Names, characters, places, and incidents are a product of the writer's imagination. All rights reserved. Scanning, uploading, and electronic sharing of this book without the permission of the author is unlawful piracy and theft. To obtain permission to excerpt portions of the text, please contact the author at katie@katielanebooks.com Thank you for respecting this author's hard work and livelihood.

Printed in the USA.

Cover Design and Interior Format
© KILLION
GROUP INC.

# Charming a BIG BAD TEXAN

KINGMAN RANCH
· 3 ·

# KATIE LANE

*To my favorite little wolf, Ridge*

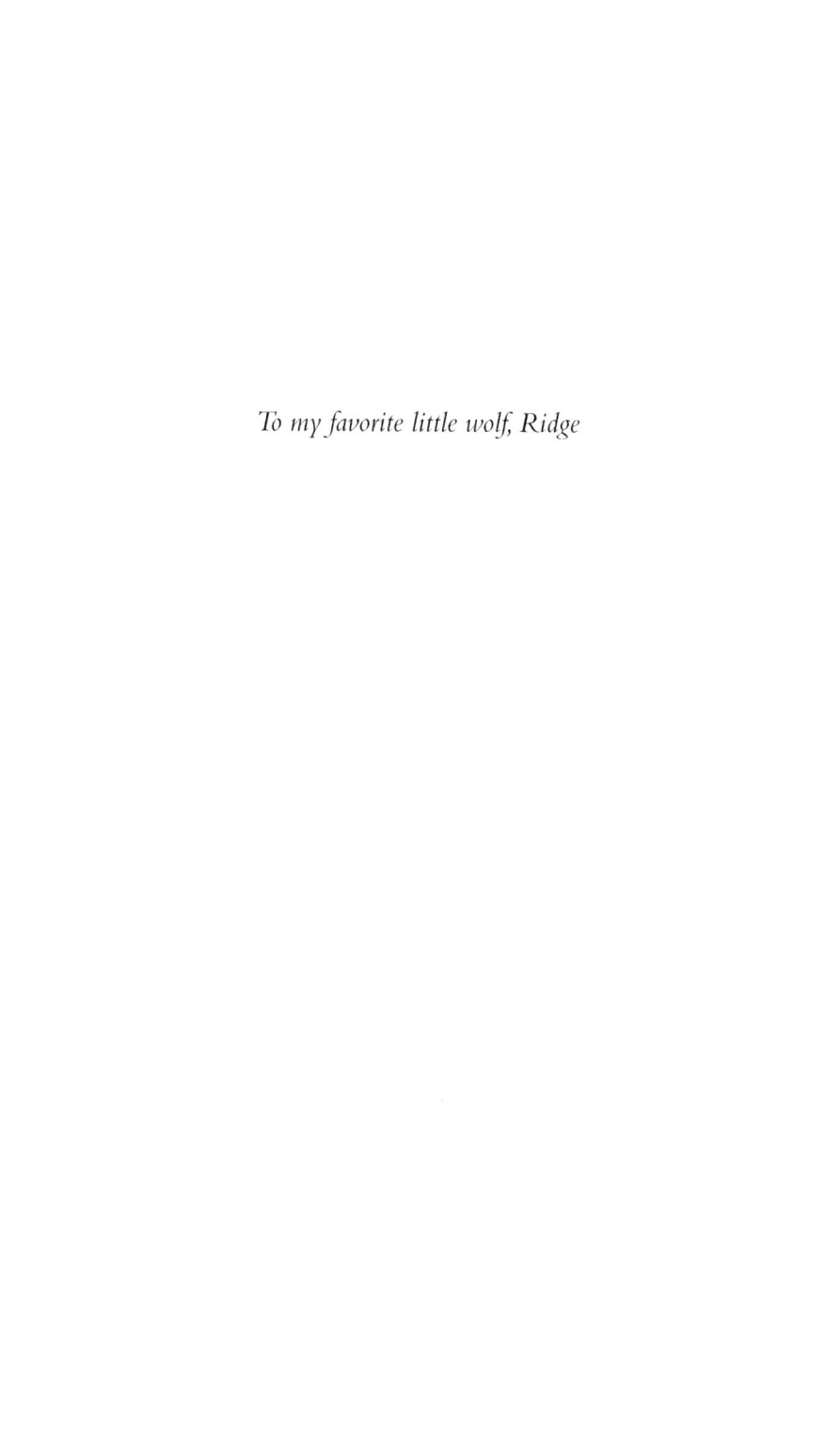

# Chapter One

Home.

As far as Gretchen Maribel Flaherty was concerned, it was the best word in the dictionary. *The place where one lives permanently, especially as a member of a family or household.*

Gretchen had never had a home. She and her mama had lived in a lot of places. But never permanently. And Mama only claimed her as family when it suited her. Consequently, Gretchen had never felt like she belonged anywhere.

Until now.

If anyone had told her that someday she'd be living in a fairy-tale castle, she would've laughed herself silly. Logical girls like Gretchen didn't dream about living in beautiful castles. They knew castles were reserved for queens and princesses. Gretchen had never been, nor would she ever be, a queen or a princess. She was just a plain ol' country gal who had inherited unruly red hair and freckles from her daddy and the gift of gab and a slow metabolism from her mama.

And yet, she'd somehow stumbled into a fairy tale—purely by accident—and was now living the dream. She still wasn't a queen or princess. She was a housekeeper. But she loved her cozy little room behind the kitchen, and she loved working for the five Kingman siblings who ran the Kingman Ranch . . . well, maybe not all five. There was one who had taken a dislike to Gretchen. He was the only one standing in the way of making Kingman Ranch her permanent home.

But she refused to ruin her night stressing about the Big Bad Wolf.

Tonight she didn't want to think about anything but enjoying her bubble bath.

The tub was huge and had a glassed in shower on one side and a tall frosted window on the other. Gretchen had lit a candle, and its flickering light danced on the shiny chrome fixtures and reflected in the bubbles clustered around her.

She sank deeper in the hot water and sighed with contentment. It just went to show you that one day you could be feeling lost and alone and the next you could be living in a castle surrounded by bubbles.

The water started to cool, and Gretchen used her toes to turn on the spigots. As she did, her heel accidentally bumped the handheld sprayer and knocked it into the tub. It turned on and a spray of water shot between Gretchen's legs, hitting a spot that had her eyes widening.

When she reached for the nozzle, rather than turn the sprayer off and put it back in its holder, she held it right where it was and let a fantasy take shape.

*The bathroom door opened and a cowboy stepped in.*

*A broad-shouldered cowboy who wore a hat low on his forehead and a black t-shirt that molded to his mountain of muscles. He moved toward her, his dusty boots clicking on the tile floor as he grew closer and closer. He pulled off his cowboy hat, revealing the thick waves of raven black hair—*

Gretchen's eyes opened and she frowned. No, not raven hair. Blond. Ordinary blond hair. She closed her eyes and returned to her fantasy.

*Tossing his hat aside, the ordinary blond cowboy knelt next to the bathtub, his smoky gray eyes—*

Her eyes flashed open again. Not smoky gray eyes. Blue eyes. Plain ol' blue eyes. She closed her eyes and tried to concentrate.

*The ordinary blond cowboy with the plain blue eyes dipped his hand beneath the bubbles and his lips lowered to her mouth as he growled . . .*

"You want me to devour you, darlin'?"

Gretchen was about to say "yes" when someone answered for her.

"Devour me, Wolfe. Please devour me."

Gretchen's eyes flashed opened and she sat up so quickly she sloshed water on the floor. But she didn't worry about the mess she'd made when the growling voice came through the door again.

"You bet, darlin'. Just give me a minute." The doorknob started to turn.

Quickly, Gretchen blew out the candles and ducked under the water. The sprayer was still on. But she couldn't turn it off without it coming out of the faucet and alerting the man who was walking in the door. So she held it under the water and prayed she could hold her breath long enough. After what felt like forever, she resurfaced.

"What the hell is the matter with you?" Wolfe said.

Figuring the jig was up, Gretchen opened her eyes and peeked over the edge of the tub. But Wolfe wasn't glaring at her. He stood at one of the double sinks with his hands braced on the granite counter. He hadn't turned on the light, but there was enough moonlight coming in the skylight for Gretchen to see him. He wore his standard black t-shirt that looked like it was painted to his chest and bulging biceps, and faded jeans that hugged his fine butt and long legs.

To say Wolfe was handsome was like saying the Mona Lisa was a nice painting. His facial features were about as perfect as a man could get without looking too feminine. His cheekbones were high. His lips were wide and full. His lashes were long and dark. With his penetrating storm-gray eyes, continual five-o'clock shadow, and wealth of wavy black hair, it was no wonder women threw themselves at his boots. The woman in the other room was no doubt waiting to do the same.

So why was Wolfe in here talking to himself?

"You can do this." He stared at his reflection. "Just relax and think about the sexy, hot woman waiting naked for you." He closed his eyes and reached for the waistband of his jeans.

Gretchen's eyes widened as he flicked open the button and lowered the zipper. They widened even more when he slipped his hand inside his underwear. A zing of desire zipped through her.

The reality playing out in front of her was twice as hot as the fantasy she'd just conjured up. She started to adjust the sprayer when Wolfe's hand dropped away and he hung his head.

"Shit."

The door opened, and Wolfe quickly straightened and zipped up his jeans as a beautiful blonde stepped in as naked as the day she was born. Wolfe hadn't lied. The woman was the definition of hot and sexy. She had full breasts that seemed to defy gravity and a flat stomach that probably had never seen a slice of chocolate cake in its life.

The woman walked over and gave Wolfe a kiss that made Gretchen's face feel hot. As she kissed him, she slid her hand over his fly. She drew away and smiled seductively.

"It feels like you could use a little warming up." She lowered to her knees.

Gretchen let out a tiny gasp, then quickly covered her mouth. But it was too late. The woman and Wolfe turned to the bathtub. The woman jumped to her feet while Wolfe walked over and switched on the light.

Gretchen squinted in the bright light and started to explain, but the woman spoke before she could. "So this is why you acted so strange when I wanted to come up to your room, Wolfe. You had another woman waiting for you."

"Oh," Gretchen said, "I'm not one of Mr. Kingman's—"

Wolfe cut her off. "Now, Sue Ann, you know I never double dip. I didn't know she'd be here. Just like I didn't know you'd follow me home from town."

The explanation and Wolfe's charming smile seemed to take all the anger right out of Sue Ann. She cuddled close to his chest. "That's all right, baby." She sent Gretchen a forced smile. "I'll just wait in the other room while you get rid of her."

Gretchen figured Wolfe would take Sue Ann up on the offer, but instead he completely surprised her. "Now, darlin'. That wouldn't be fair. Not when she was here first."

Sue Ann's eyes widened. "Are you saying you choose that red-headed cow over me?"

Gretchen stiffened. "Red-headed cow? Now wait one—"

Wolfe held up his hands. "Ladies, ladies, there's no need to fight. What do you say we call it a draw and I don't sleep with either one of you tonight?"

"A draw?" Sue Ann released a loud, angry *humph* before she stormed out of the bathroom, slamming the door behind her. When she was gone, Wolfe slowly turned to Gretchen. The charming smile was gone, replaced with the same annoyed, confused look he always gave her—like she was a cold sore that had popped up out of nowhere and he couldn't figure out how to get rid of.

Wolfe was the only Kingman who didn't like her. In fact, he'd made no bones about wanting her fired. And she couldn't blame him. The more she tried to make him like her, the more klutzy she became.

She had spilled coffee, sweet tea, soup, and a variety of other liquids on him. She'd walked in on him when he was showering, lost his socks in the laundry, vacuumed up his Airpods . . . and even set fire to his bed. None of it had been intentional. But he didn't seem to believe that. If it were up to him, Gretchen would've been long gone by now.

She didn't want to go.

The Kingman Ranch was her home.

"I am so sorry, sir," she said as she sunk lower in the bubbles that seem to be popping as she spoke. "I didn't mean to mess up your . . . evening. You see, the faucet in my bathtub sprung a leak. Your sister Adeline said I could use one of the bathrooms upstairs until the plumber can get here on Monday to fix mine. And since you were in Amarillo lookin' at horses and your bathroom had this big ol' tub that wasn't being used, I thought you wouldn't mind if—"

He cut her off. "But I do mind, Miss Flaherty. I mind a lot. I have repeatedly asked you to stay out of my room and repeatedly you have ignored me."

"But I'm the housekeeper, Mr. Kingman. I have to supervise the maids and make sure your room is being cleaned properly. It's my job."

"And what does walking in while I'm showering have to do with making sure my room is clean?"

Her face flushed at the memory of seeing his naked body all soaped up. "I was just putting fresh towels in your bathroom. The door wasn't locked. Although there must be something wrong with that latch because I locked it tonight and you walked right in." She smiled brightly. "So I guess that makes us even."

He spoke through gritted teeth. "Not even close. I want you to stay away from me. I don't want you in my room. I don't want you in my bathroom. And I don't want you in my tub. Do I make myself clear?"

"Yes, sir!" She went to do a little salute, forgetting about the spray nozzle in her hand. As soon as it was out of the tub, water shot through the air ... and hit Wolfe right in the face.

"Oh, no!" Gretchen gasped as she tried to find the shut off button. When she couldn't, she pulled it back under the water and sat up to turn off the taps.

But it was too late.

By the time she looked back, Wolfe was wet from his thick raven hair to his lizard-skin boots. His jaw worked back and forth like he was a cow chewing on a nasty piece of cud. Then his gaze lowered, and his jaw stopped moving and dropped open.

When Gretchen glanced down, she understood why. Her boobs were no longer covered in bubbles. They hung there like two huge water balloons. She released a little squeal before she crossed her arms over her chest and slid back in the tub, sloshing even more water onto the floor.

For a long, embarrassing moment, Wolfe stood there staring at the water with its thin layer of bubbles before he turned on a boot heel and walked out, slamming the door behind him.

Once he was gone, Gretchen quickly got out

of the tub and dried off with a towel. "You've done it now, Gretchen Maribel Flaherty. If this doesn't get you fired, nothing will." She pulled on her chenille robe and hurried out of the en suite bathroom, hoping to apologize . . . but she was struck speechless by the sight of a shirtless Wolfe stripping off his wet jeans.

Just like when she'd walked in on him taking a shower, she became paralyzed by his masculine beauty. By the artfully arranged muscles. The perfect sprinkling of dark hair. And the sexy snarling wolf tattoo. All she could do was stand there ogling him like a Magic Mike strip show. If she'd had any dollars, it would've been raining money.

Unfortunately, he didn't appreciate her appreciation. When he noticed her, he jerked his jeans back up and released a growl. "Out!"

She scurried out of the room like a scared mouse and ran into Adeline coming out of her bedroom. If anyone was a princess, Adeline Kingman was. She was beautiful and kind and gracious. She never treated Gretchen like an employee. She'd always treated her like a friend.

"Gretchen, what happened? Is that Wolfe I heard yelling?"

Gretchen nodded. "He came home from Amarillo early . . . and caught me taking a bubble bath in his tub. I'm so sorry, Addie. I should've used one of the guest bathrooms."

Adeline waved a hand. "You didn't know he was going to come home early." She laughed. "Although you certainly know how to get under my brother's skin."

Gretchen's shoulders slumped. "He hates me."

"He doesn't hate you. He just isn't used to women being so . . ."

"Klutzy around him. Everything I do for him turns out wrong."

Adeline smiled. "Maybe that's not a bad thing. Wolfe has too many women wrapped around his little finger as is."

"But I'm sure he'll want you to fire me after this."

"This house is my domain. No one can tell me who to hire or fire." Adeline gave her a hug. "So stop worrying. You're not going anywhere. You're not only a wonderful housekeeper, you're my friend. And I'm thankful every day that you answered that ad."

Gretchen hadn't intended to answer the online ad. She hadn't come to the Kingman Ranch to be a housekeeper. She'd just wanted to see the castle her mama had talked about. When Adeline had made the wrong assumption, Gretchen had gone along with it. It was the best decision she'd ever made.

"I'm thankful every day too." She hugged Adeline tight. But despite Adeline's assurance, Gretchen knew that blood was thicker than water. If she couldn't figure out a way to get Wolfe to like her, there was a possibility she might get fired.

"Everything okay, sweetheart?" The bedroom door opened and Adeline's husband appeared. Gage Reardon was the ranch foreman and as handsome as all the other cowboys on the ranch.

"Everything is fine," Adeline said. "Gretchen

and I were just having a girl moment." She sent Gage a loving look. "But now that you're awake . . ."

Gretchen took her cue. "Goodnight, y'all. See you in the mornin'."

Once downstairs, she checked to make sure all the lights were off and the doors locked before she headed to her room. On the way, she passed through the kitchen. With its eight-burner gas stove, three ovens, a commercial-sized refrigerator, and a marble-topped island perfect for rolling out piecrust, it was her dream kitchen.

Gretchen didn't have a lot of talents. One talent she did have was making pies. But since coming to the Kingman Ranch, she had to put her love of baking aside. The Kingmans' cook, Potts, was an old chuck wagon cowboy who didn't like people messing in his kitchen.

She stopped by the marble island and glanced around. What would it hurt if she made one little ol' pie?

One little ol' pie to win over a big, bad wolf.

## Chapter Two

THE SUN HAD yet to peek its head over the horizon when Wolfe woke up. Most people thought he was a bad boy who loved to carouse all night and sleep all day. And he did love to carouse at night. But he also loved the early mornings when the hustle of a working ranch had yet to start and the air coming in the open window smelled of horse manure and dew-drenched grass.

Wolfe had always had a sensitive sniffer. This morning, he detected another scent in the air. The scent of something good baking. And Wolfe loved food almost as much as he loved women . . . although recently his desire for women had dwindled.

For some reason, he was having trouble getting an erection. The problem had started a few weeks earlier. He figured it had to do with boredom. He had always prided himself on living a wild, exciting life. But his wild exploits had taken on a sameness that had started to bore him to tears. Bar fights didn't get his adrenaline pumping anymore. And neither did spending time with women.

The only spark of excitement he'd felt in the last month had come from an unlikely source. One he wasn't about to consider. But it had proved that things were still working. Which was a relief.

His stomach growled, and he rolled out of bed and got dressed.

In the kitchen, he expected to see Potts making whatever smelled so damn good. But the cook was nowhere in sight. Wolfe sniffed and glanced around until he spotted a pie sitting on the counter.

It was about the prettiest thing he'd ever seen in his life. The crust was a golden brown and laced in perfect overlapping strips on top of a glossy sunshine peach filling.

Wolfe was ravenous . . . and confused. Potts never made pies. He made cakes, crumbles, cobblers, and all kinds of other desserts, but never pies. At least not since Wolfe's mother had passed away. Elizabeth Kingman had loved pie. Wolfe had been too young at her passing to remember much about his mother, but according to his brother Stetson, she could eat an entire apple pie all by herself.

It turned out Wolfe had inherited the same ability. He'd only planned to eat a slice of the peach pie. But once the flaky, buttery crust and sweet, brown-sugary peaches melted on his tongue, he couldn't seem to control himself. Before he knew it, there were only a few flakes and a smear of peach filling left in the pie plate.

Potts was going to kill him. Not to mention his brothers and sisters . . . but only if they caught him. Luckily, it was Sunday and everyone got up late. He quickly tossed the evidence in the trash and headed out the door.

The sun had risen, casting the entire ranch in its warm glow. A herd of cattle in a nearby pasture lowed while hungry horses in the stables whinnied. In the distance, an owl hooted its goodnight. A few seconds later, a rooster welcomed the day.

The door of the bunkhouse opened and the herding dogs, Raleigh and Dex, raced out to do their morning business. When they were finished, they ran over to Wolfe for a good ear scratch.

"Hey boys, you two staying out of trouble?"

They followed him to the stable door before racing back to the bunkhouse for any bacon scraps the bunkhouse cook might slip into their food bowls.

Wolfe punched in the security code on the stable door. There was a time that all you had to do to get into the stables was slide open two wooden doors. Now the doors were steel and rumbled as they drew apart automatically.

There had also been a time when the stable manager hadn't greeted you with a shotgun.

Wolfe held up his hands. "It's just me, Tab."

Tab lowered the gun. "Sorry, Wolfe. Just being cautious. Of course, now that Jasper is dead, I guess there's no need for it."

The mention of his cousin put a damper on Wolfe's good mood. He had been trying not to think about Jasper since the fire that killed him. But every time Wolfe turned around there was some reminder.

Jasper had been Wolfe's second cousin . . . and his friend. Even though Wolfe lived on the Kingman Ranch and Jasper had lived in town, they'd had more in common than Wolfe had with his own brothers. They were the black sheep of their families. The ones who never quite met the high expectations of the Kingman name. They hadn't excelled at school or sports. They hadn't excelled at business or ranching. They'd both just been drifting through life with no purpose except having fun.

Or so Wolfe had thought.

But it turned out Jasper hadn't just been drifting through life with no purpose. He'd had a purpose: Get even with his cousins for inheriting the Kingman Ranch when he thought a share of it should've been his. Wolfe had been unaware of Jasper's desire to own the ranch. He hadn't seen the troubled soul beneath the easygoing smile—or the unstable criminal, who could mutilate a bull, set fire to a barn, attack Tab and Wolfe's sister-in-law Lily, and try to kill Adeline and Stetson.

Just the thought of Jasper trying to kill his family made Wolfe want to hit something.

"You okay, Wolfe?"

Tab's question brought Wolfe out of his thoughts. He unclenched his fists and smiled. "Yeah. I'm fine."

"You want me to saddle up a horse for you?"

"Actually, I wanted to check on that horse I brought in last night."

Tab chuckled. "I don't know if I'd call that animal a horse. He reminds me of a mutt dog my daddy owned. Ugliest thing you ever did see."

Wolfe couldn't argue. Especially when Tab led the horse out of a stall. The horse was a buckskin color with splotches of mottled gray on his rump. His ears were oversized and fly-bitten. His front legs had bowed tendons. And he was grossly overweight. Compared to the thoroughbred cutting and racehorses the ranch bred, the poor animal did look like a stray mutt.

Stetson was going to be pissed. He had sent Wolfe to Amarillo for a new stud and Wolfe had brought home this pathetic animal. But the horse had a sweet nature. As soon as he saw Wolfe, he came over and plopped his head on Wolfe's shoulder. Almost as if he was staying thank you for being given such a nice home.

Wolfe stroked the horse's neck. "You like it here, boy? Did Tab give you enough breakfast to fill your big—?"

"What the hell is that?"

Wolfe turned to see Stetson striding into the stables. Stet stared at the horse as if he was seeing things. There was nothing Wolfe loved more than surprising his big brother. He kept his arm around the horse and grinned.

"This here is Sir Galahad. But I think I'm going to call him Mutt." He winked at Tab. "Mutt's our new stud."

Stetson's eyes narrowed in anger. "This is the stud you bought at the auction?"

Wolfe hadn't bought the horse at the auction. He'd won him from an old cowboy in a poker game. But he figured his brother didn't need to know that. "He might not look like much, but his previous owner said he was the best cutting horse in Texas. And he's registered and has a good bloodline."

"If that sad excuse for an animal came from good stock, I'll eat my friggin' hat." Stetson whipped off his hat and slapped it against his leg. "Delaney brings home some pretty pathetic animals, but I never thought you were the type to buy with your heart instead of your head."

Wolfe gave the horse's neck a pat. "Now, come on, Stet. You have to admit Mutt is kinda cute." As if on cue, Mutt pulled back his lips and gave Stetson a big toothy grin. Wolfe laughed, but Stetson only rolled his eyes.

"The price of his feed will come out of your pocket. From the looks of him, that won't be cheap." Stetson tugged on his hat. "And have the vet look him over to make sure the mangy thing doesn't have any parasites or diseases."

"Who has parasites and diseases?" Lily walked into the stables. Stetson's angry look immediately softened when he saw his wife. If anyone had told Wolfe months ago that a little slip of a woman would change his big brother's sour disposition, he wouldn't have believed them. But the proof was there for all to see as Stetson tucked a protective arm around Lily.

"Wolfe bought a new horse . . . if that's what you'd call that thing."

Lily glanced over at Mutt. Her eyes widened. "He looks . . . umm . . . nice."

"See?" Wolfe winked at his sister-in-law. "Lily

knows good horseflesh when she sees it. What has you two up so early?"

"I have a book signing in Houston," Lily said. "And I talked Stetson into coming with me so we can have a little mini vacation." Lily was a best-selling author of a popular children's book series called Fairy Prairie. As the gardener's daughter, she had grown up on the ranch and had known the Kingmans for most of her life. "You're welcome to come too, Wolfe."

"Thanks for the offer, Lil," he said. "But seeing as you and Stet are still newlyweds, I think I'll pass. How long are you going to be gone?"

"We'll be back on Tuesday." Stetson sent Wolfe a warning look. "Try to stay out of trouble." Wolfe didn't take offense at the warning. Trouble did seem to find him . . . when he didn't go looking for it.

He shrugged. "I'll do my best, big brother."

Once Stetson and Lily left the stables, Wolfe and Tab set up a nutrition and exercise program for Mutt. With his tendon issues, the horse couldn't be ridden for a while so it would be impossible to prove if the old cowboy had been right. But Wolfe seriously doubted Mutt was a champion cutting horse. Still, he planned to look Sir Galahad up on the Internet. Wolfe stayed to make sure Mutt was comfortable before he headed back to the house.

Most people thought the Kingman castle was an ostentatious monstrosity that belonged in a storybook rather than in the middle of Texas. As Wolfe walked toward the huge stone structure with its tall turrets, he figured they were probably right. But like Wolfe, Grandpa King had enjoyed surprising people and doing the unexpected. Building a castle complete with an English garden in the middle of a cattle and horse ranch was unexpected.

But just because people lived in a castle didn't mean they acted like royalty. As soon as Wolfe stepped in the kitchen from the mudroom, he heard his little sister and brother going at it. While most twins were inseparable, Delaney and Buck preferred to be separated. When they weren't, they fought like cats and dogs.

"You are a no-good lying sneak, Buck Kingman," Delaney said. "My eggs were right there on my plate and now they're gone."

"How do you know it was me?" Buck asked. "It could've been that mangy barn cat you insist on bringing into the house."

"Millie would never do something like that. She's not gluttonous like my brothers."

"Brothers?" Wolfe moved into the room and pulled out a chair at the table. "I wasn't even here. There's no way I could've stolen your eggs, Del." As he sat down, he grabbed a piece of toast from Delaney's plate. After the pie, he wasn't really that hungry. But he loved razzing his little sister.

"See!" She jerked the toast back before he could take a bite. "It's a wonder I get to eat at all."

"Everyone in this family eats more than a herd of starving buffalo. Even Adeline's appetite has improved since she married Gage." Potts walked over to the table and exchanged an empty platter for one filled with fluffy eggs mixed with onions and red bell pepper. Maybe Wolfe could eat a little more. He waited for Potts to say something about the pie, but the cook only asked, "Where are Addie and Gage?"

"Probably having some rowdy morning sex," Delaney said with her usual bluntness. "Which is what I wish I was doing."

"Good God, Del!" Buck covered his ears. "It's Sunday, for Christ's sake."

"God was the one who created sex in the first place. I'm sure He won't be mad at Addie and Gage for enjoying it. Or at me for wishing I was enjoying it." She scowled. "But I can't even get a kiss on the cheek because every man in the county is terrified of my brothers."

"Don't blame it on us," Buck said as he scooped up some eggs. "Men are more likely terrified of an aggressive, over-achieving know-it-all who thinks she can outride, out-shoot, and out-rope every cowboy in the state of Texas."

Delaney shrugged and took a bite of her eggs. "Because I can."

Wolfe grinned. "Don't you ever change, Delly Belly. If a man doesn't like you for who you are, then you don't want him."

Delaney's brows knitted and she lowered her fork. "Except not one man seems to like me for who I am."

"One will. I promise." He helped himself to some eggs.

"That's easy for you to say. Every woman in town likes you for who you are. They don't even seem to care that you go through them like a raccoon picking through trash."

"Now wait a second, Del. I don't treat women like—"

"Good mornin'!"

Gretchen Flaherty sailed into the kitchen with a bright smile on her face. Last night, her hair had been piled on top of her head in a mass of wet curls. This morning, it was pulled tight in a single long braid that trailed all the way down to her waist. She always wore loose dresses. Until last night, Wolfe hadn't known what they hid. He wished he didn't know now. As she glanced around the kitchen as if looking for something, he couldn't seem to keep his gaze off her breasts . . . and remember how they looked all water-slick and hanging like pale overripe fruit topped with large raspberry-colored nipples the size of silver dollars.

Just like that, his penis woke up and made its presence known.

"Oh, hell no."

He hadn't realized he'd spoken out loud until everyone turned to him.

"Hell no what?" Delaney asked.

He cleared his throat. "Hell no I . . . don't want any coffee, Potts."

Potts turned from the stove and stared at him as if he had gone crazy. "I didn't offer you any."

"Well, I just wanted to let you know I don't want any in case you were going to offer me some."

Potts turned back to the stove and shook his

head. "Darn crazy family. I'd be better off working at a IHOP."

"Are you headed to church, Gretchen?" Delaney asked.

"I sure am. Do you want to come? Reverend Floyd will be retiring soon so you only have a few more Sundays to hear him preach."

"Didn't Reverend Floyd's son have a crush on you, Del?" Buck asked. "There's a man for you."

Delaney rolled her eyes. "Thanks a lot. But I don't want some goody-goody preacher's son as my first lover. I want a stud who knows his way around a bedroom."

Buck sighed and looked up at the ceiling. "Forgive her, Lord. She knows not what she says."

"I know exactly what I said. If I'm going to sow some wild oats I want to do it with a bad boy who has no problem getting it up."

Wolfe choked on the eggs he'd just swallowed. Before he could clear his throat, Gretchen released a startled "Oh!"

He shot a glance over at her and found her studying him with a look in her shamrock eyes that said she'd just put all the pieces of a puzzle together.

Damn.

# Chapter Three

GRETCHEN HADN'T GIVEN much thought to what Wolfe had been doing in the bathroom before Sue Ann came in . . . until Delaney mentioned she was looking for a bad boy who had no trouble getting it up and Wolfe choked. Then everything had become crystal clear.

Wolfe Kingman was a bad boy who couldn't get it up.

If she had kept her big mouth shut and hadn't released a surprised "oh," he never would've known that she knew. But she had, and those gray eyes zeroed in on her.

"Is something wrong, Miss Flaherty?" he asked.

"No, sir." She shook her head. "Nothing's wrong." She forced a smile. "I just realized I'm going to be late for church if I don't hurry." She started for the back door, but Wolfe got up from the table and blocked her exit.

"How about I drive you to church, Miss Flaherty? There are a few things I need to pick up in town anyway."

"Oh, that's okay. I'm fine driving my—"

"But I insist," he said in a low growl. He ushered her out the door to the six-car garage where his black dually truck was parked. He opened the passenger door and waited for her to climb in.

Since it didn't look like she had much choice, she stepped up on the running board and grabbed the handle to pull herself onto the high seat. Unfortunately, nerves had made her palms sweaty and her hand slipped and she fell backwards. Wolfe caught her, but not before she smacked him hard in the face with the bible in her other hand.

"Oh, Mr. Kingman. I'm so sorry. Are you hurt?"

Without answering, he lifted her onto the seat as if she weighed no more than a bag of potatoes. He slammed the door and headed around to the other side. He didn't say anything as he started the truck and opened the garage. Silence had always made Gretchen uncomfortable.

"It sure is a pretty day, isn't it?" she said as they pulled out into the bright sunshine. "It doesn't seem like fall at all. It seems more like—"

He cut her off. "What did you see last night?"

She swallowed hard. "See? I didn't see a thing."

He glanced over at her, his gray eyes piercing. "Are you sure, Miss Flaherty? And this time before you lie, you might want to look where your hand is placed."

Gretchen glanced down at her hand on her bible and cringed. Now she had to tell the truth. She knew the truth was not going to endear her to Wolfe Kingman. She didn't even have a pie to gift him. Last night, she had left the peach pie cooling on the counter, and this morning, it had been gone. It looked like fate was against her winning Wolfe's favor.

She sighed. "I did see a little something last night." When Wolfe's eyebrows popped up, she realized how that sounded. "I don't mean that what I saw was little. I didn't see . . . it at all. I just saw you putting your hand . . . ." Try as she might she couldn't stop herself from glancing down. His jeans looked as soft as butter and seemed to cup the bulge between his muscled thighs perfectly.

He cleared his throat, and she lifted her gaze to find him scowling. "Sorry," she said. "What was I saying?"

He looked back at the road. "I don't have a problem getting it up if that's what you're thinking."

"Of course not." She paused. "But if you did, it wouldn't be anything to worry about. Stepdaddy Number Four had the same problem and the doc gave him a prescription for it and once he started taking it, Mama was happy as a pig in mud—of course, she still left Bernie. But it had nothing to do with getting it up. It had more to do with him cutting her off from using his credit card."

Gretchen thought she'd said exactly the right thing. But Wolfe didn't look relieved. He looked like he wanted to strangle the steering wheel. Or maybe her.

"I don't need Viagra to make women happy. What you saw last night was just a . . . fluke. I was tired after the drive from Amarillo. Absolutely nothing is wrong with me. So don't be spreading rumors around town that there is."

She could understand his concern. If word got

out Wolfe Kingman couldn't get an erection, it would certainly cause a ruckus. Women would be devastated. And men would probably be thrilled he was no longer in competition. Not to mention what it would do to Wolfe. Her mama had always said a man's ego was directly connected to his penis. Given Wolfe's knitted brow and stranglehold on the steering wheel, that seemed to be true.

"I would never spread rumors about you, Mr. Kingman." She held up her three fingers. "I give you my Brownie oath." Even though she'd been kicked out of Brownies for eating all the boxes of cookies she'd sold, she still respected the oath. "What happens on the Kingman Ranch stays on the Kingman Ranch."

He studied her for a long moment before he returned his attention to the highway. "Somehow I doubt that."

His lack of trust in her wasn't surprising. Every time she tried to prove her worth to him it turned into a disaster. But she wasn't going to stop trying.

"I'm not good at a lot of things, but keepin' secrets is one of them. So you don't have to worry that anyone will find out about your . . . little problem. Although not being able to have sex isn't really a problem. Take me for instance. I haven't had sex in over two years and I don't even miss it. It turned out Gary Don breaking up with me was a blessing in disguise. It made me want to leave Arkansas so I didn't have to see him with his new girlfriend. Look at me now. I'm working in a big castle for the nicest family in Texas and I finally have a best friend. Adeline is about the best friend a girl could ask for. So what I'm saying, Mr. Kingman, is that maybe what you think is the worst thing to happen to you will turn out to be the best."

She thought it was a nice little pep talk, but it turned out to be a waste of time. Wolfe only seemed to focus on one thing.

"You haven't had sex in over two years?"

"Well, yes, but that wasn't the point I was trying to make. I was trying to say that sometimes bad things that happen to you are really blessings in—"

"Wait a second." He shot a glance over at her. There was a wicked twinkle in his gray eyes that left her feeling a little breathless. "That's what you were doing last night with the sprayer. You were masturbating."

Her face flamed with heat, and she quickly took her hand off the bible. "No I wasn't."

He laughed. "Liar."

She turned away from his twinkling eyes and sat there with her face burning and nothing to say. Unfortunately, he suddenly seemed to have plenty.

"Why have you gone so long without sex? I guess this Gerry Joe broke your heart."

"Gary Don."

He snorted. "His name screams asshole." She couldn't help but smile as he continued. "I say forget him and move on. I'm sure you'll find Mr. Right if you keep looking."

"I'm not looking for Mr. Right."

He glanced over. "Put your hand back on the bible and repeat that. I've discovered that most woman are looking for Mr. Right."

She placed her hand back on the bible. "I'm not. Gary Don was my one attempt at finding Mr. Right." She refused to be like her mama and spend her life marrying one Mr. Wrong after the other. "I'm quite content without a man."

A smirk tipped up his lips. "All you need is a bathtub sprayer."

Gretchen's face flamed once again. It was a relief when the *Welcome to Cursed. Stay at your own risk.* sign came into view.

When her mama had first told her about Cursed, Texas, Gretchen had thought she was being facetious. Her mama did not like small towns. Which was why they had never lived in one. But when Gretchen first drove through the town, she realized her mama hadn't been kidding.

Cursed had been named for all the calamities that had beset the first settlers. Those folks must have been made out of sturdy stock because they didn't let tornadoes, drought, pestilence, and other hardships keep them down. They were proud of their perseverance and even named the streets of the town after all the trials they lived through. The present townsfolk were just as proud and put the town's name on everything from the Cursed Seed and Feed to the Cursed Grocery Market. The only ladies club in town was even called the Cursed Ladies' Auxiliary.

The only businesses not labeled with the name

were the restaurant, bar, and church. Gretchen figured that keeping "cursed" out of the name of a church was probably a good thing.

The people streaming in the doors of the Holy Gospel church stopped and stared as Wolfe pulled into the parking lot and parked next to the curb. But he was either used to it or didn't seem to notice as he got out and came around to open her door. When she teetered on the running board, he sighed and effortlessly lifted her down to the sidewalk.

A tingle of sexual awareness ran through her, but she thought nothing of it. What woman wouldn't be sexually aware of Wolfe Kingman? His shoulders beneath her palms were broad and muscled. His hands on her waist were gentle but strong. And his stormy gray eyes promised things—naughty things—that stole a woman's breath right out of her lungs.

"You keep my secret, Miss Flaherty," he said in a low, husky voice, "and I'll keep yours." He winked.

While Gretchen was trying to catch her balance, Mystic Malone came walking towards them. Mystic ran the Cursed Cut and Curl hair salon. She always wore fashionable clothes that looked perfect on her petite body and a short hairstyle that complimented her pixie features.

"Has Hell frozen over?"

Wolfe grinned from ear to ear as he scooped Mystic up in his arms. The two could have been brother and sister with their jet-black hair and handsome features. "No, Hell did not freeze over,

Squirt. I'm not staying for church. I'm just dropping off Gretchen."

It was the first time he'd called her by her first name. He usually called her Miss Flaherty. Or "that woman." Gretchen couldn't help feeling pleased. Maybe driving into town together had helped him warm up to her. Maybe all she needed to do to get him to like her was exchange more secrets.

"Hey, Gretchen." Mystic pointed a finger at Wolfe. "You better watch out or your reputation with be ruined hanging out with this bad boy."

"Thus says a bad girl," Wolfe teased. He glanced around. "Now I better get out of here before Hell does freeze over."

"I think you're more worried about lightning striking you dead," Mystic said.

He laughed and ruffled her hair. "Damn right I am. Which is why I was hoping you could give Gretchen a ride back to the ranch after church. Maybe you could do a little horseback riding with my ornery brother. I think he misses you since you've become so busy with your salon."

Something sad passed over Mystic's face, but it was replaced so quickly with a bright smile Gretchen figured she had imagined it. "I'd be happy to drive Gretchen back to the ranch."

"Great. When you come, I'll show you the new thoroughbred I bought." He laughed as if he'd said something funny before he looked at Gretchen. "I guess I'll see you later."

"Thank you for the ride . . ." She tried using his first name to see how he'd react. "Wolfe."

He didn't react at all. He just nodded and headed around his truck to the driver's side. The truck was as black as his hair and t-shirt. As a kid, she'd always dreamed of a white knight coming to her rescue, but as she watched Wolfe drive away, she had to admit there was something dangerously appealing about a bad boy in black.

"Hey, Mystic!" Kitty Carson came hustling over, pulling a man in a brown cowboy hat behind her. Kitty delivered the mail to the townsfolk of Cursed, along with all the town gossip. She was a short, stout, middle-aged woman with hair much redder and shorter than Gretchen's. "This here is Reverend Ransom. He's applying for the position of pastor now that Reverend Floyd is retiring."

The man took off his hat. He didn't look like a preacher. Preachers were usually all spit and polish. This man looked like he'd just come off a long cattle drive. His shaggy blond hair needed a good cut. His scruffy beard needed a good trim. And his wrinkled western shirt needed a good ironing.

"Reverend Ransom, this is Mystic Malone, who owns the beauty salon and has been a member of our community since birth." Kitty glanced at Gretchen. "And this is Gretchen Flaherty, who works for the Kingmans, one of our most prestigious families. The reverend here is single and I was just telling him what fine-looking young ladies we had for him to choose from."

Mystic slipped an arm through Gretchen's. "And we'd be happy to show you our teeth so you can see if we're good breeding stock, Reverend Ransom."

The reverend tipped back his head and laughed before he sent them a flirty grin. "It's a pleasure to meet you ladies. Miss Kitty was right. There are some beautiful women here in Cursed. I'm thinking this town should be called Blessed."

Gretchen blushed and was about to reply with a thank you when Mystic's grandmother, Hester Malone, walked up. Hester was the resident palm reader and fortuneteller. Gretchen had never believed people could tell the future . . . until Hester had foreseen Jasper causing trouble for the Kingman Ranch. After that prophecy, Gretchen was a believer . . . and more than a little wary of Hester. Especially when she stared the way she was staring at the reverend. Intently. Like she was reading his innermost thoughts.

"So you're the new preacher, are you? Funny, but I'm not getting a godly vibe."

"And just how would you know anything about godly vibes, Hester Malone?" Kitty asked. "Last time I checked, palm readin' and fortune tellin' isn't in the bible."

Hester turned on Kitty. The two women didn't seem to like each other. Every time Gretchen had seen them together, sparks flew. "Then you haven't read the bible. What do you think prophecy is if not forecasting the future, Gossip Girl?"

"I don't gossip! Just like you don't forecast the future. You told Danielle Jonas that she was going to inherit a fortune from her great aunt and all she inherited was her aunt's sickly cat."

"To some people, animals are worth a fortune.

And you better watch how you talk to me, Kitty." Hester fingered the purple crystal hanging from a chain around her neck and narrowed her eyes at Kitty. But before any hexes could go flying, Mystic stepped in.

"That's enough, Hessy. You and Kitty quit arguing in front of the reverend. If we're not careful, he'll go running for the hills."

Reverend Ransom smiled. "I've never been much of a runner." He bent his elbow. "Ms. Kitty, should we go inside and find our seats?"

Kitty gave Hester one more snide look before she took the pastor's arm and allowed him to lead her away.

When they were gone, Hester spoke. "One day, that woman is going to get what she deserves. Of course, it might be today. I didn't see a halo over that man's head. But I did see a pair of horns."

"Stop it, Hessy," Mystic warned.

Hester waved a hand. "You might ignore your gift, but I refuse to ignore mine." Her gaze landed on Gretchen, and a chill ran down Gretchen's spine. "And you're hiding something too."

Gretchen couldn't reply as fear tightened her throat.

"I don't see what you're hiding, but I do see what you want." Hester stroked the crystal. "And you'll find true love, Gretchen Flaherty." She smiled. "In the least likely place."

# Chapter Four

AFTER LEAVING THE church, Wolfe started to worry that he'd made a big mistake by leaving Gretchen there. Holy Gospel was also known as Holy Gossip. It would be the perfect place for her to spread the news about what she'd seen last night. Regardless of the oath she'd taken, he couldn't see her keeping her mouth shut. The woman talked more than any woman he'd met in his life.

In just the short drive to town, she had shared way too much information.

Like the entire two years without sex thing. He didn't need to know about Gretchen's sex life. He didn't want to think about Gretchen and sex at all.

And yet . . . his mind kept going down that path. When it did, his cock jumped to attention. Like at breakfast when the image of her naked breasts had popped into his head. In the truck when she'd stared at his crotch. When he realized what she had been doing with the sprayer. And when he lifted her down to the sidewalk in front of the church and had gotten lost in her pretty emerald eyes.

Even now, just rehashing the thoughts, he grew hard. It pissed him off. He couldn't get it up with other women, and yet he could just think about Gretchen—a woman who terrified the hell out of him—and he got an erection.

Every time he turned around, she was there, spilling something on him or cracking him in the head with a mop handle or spraying him in the face with water. She was the last person in the world he would take to bed. Not only because he worried about the safety of his private parts, but also because she wasn't his type.

No matter what she said about being happy without a man, Gretchen was one of those starry-eyed women who had a hope chest filled with Grandma's quilts and Aunt Sophie's silver candlestick holders and Mama's wedding dress—or dresses, it sounded like. The kind who was looking for a happily ever after.

Wolfe didn't do happy ever afters. He enjoyed being with women. But he wasn't about to make a commitment to one that he couldn't keep. Wolfe knew he was selfish. He was more interested in having fun than being responsible. But he wasn't selfish enough to make a commitment to a woman and then freeze her out. Which was why he had no desire to get married. Or even get in a serious relationship.

He wasn't looking for love. Just a good time.

Although, recently, he hadn't been having such a good time. A dark cloud hung over him. It wasn't just boredom or the trouble he was having with his libido. It was something else. When Nasty Jack's bar came into view, he couldn't stop the anger that welled up inside him. As usual, Uncle Jack's Cadillac was parked in the parking space by the bar's front door. Unable to stop himself, Wolfe veered into the parking lot and parked next to the Cadillac.

The front door wasn't locked, and Wolfe shoved his way in, the door cracking against the old cigarette machine in the entryway. Inside was as dark as it always was. The only light came from the colored Christmas lights above the bar, the beer signs covering the walls, and the bright green Exit sign at the back.

A thick ball of emotion swelled up in Wolfe's throat as he glanced at the bar. As mad as he was at Jasper, he missed his cousin's bright smile and "Hey, cuz!" Missed it so bad it hurt.

"What the hell do you want?"

Pulling his gaze from the bar, Wolfe headed to the back table where his uncle sat. Uncle Jack was around eighty with thinning white hair and dark brown eyes that Wolfe had never seen hold anything but anger and meanness.

Today was no different.

He glared at Wolfe, his loose jowls shaking as he spoke. "Well, answer the question, boy. What the hell are you doing here?"

Wolfe rested his hands on the table and spoke in a low growl. "You were the one who soured Jasper on us, weren't you, old man? You might've acted all innocent with the sheriff, but I know you were the one who poisoned Jasper's mind with thoughts of revenge. All because you blamed your brother for stealing your family's land."

Uncle Jack slammed his fist on the table, causing the glass to jump and spill whiskey. "Because the bastard did! The Kingman Ranch would be half mine if not for your conniving, cheating grandfather."

Wolfe jabbed a finger at him. "My grandfather bought the land from you fair and square."

"Is that the bullshit he told your family? That he bought the land fair and square?" Uncle Jack snorted. "There was nothing fair and square about your grandfather. He tricked me into selling him my land just like he tricked your mama out of hers."

Wolfe straightened. "What are you talking about?"

Uncle Jack studied him for a minute before he looked away and picked up his whiskey. "It doesn't matter anymore. Believe what you will." He downed the whiskey and got up. "You want to rob me blind like your granddaddy, go right ahead. Now that's Jasper's gone, I'll have to close the bar anyway." He turned and headed to the stairs leading to the upper floor in a shuffling, limping gait that made Wolfe realize just how old he was.

The anger drained out of Wolfe, and he flopped down in a chair and ran a hand over his face. What was he doing threatening an old man who could barely walk? He shouldn't be here. But for some reason he couldn't seem to leave. He thought about what Jack had said. Was he right?

Had King cheated Jack out of land and Wolfe's mother too? Wolfe couldn't remember his grandfather. But his father, Douglas, had often ranted about how land hungry his own father had been. Was it possible Uncle Jack's hatred was justified? And Jasper's?

As if conjuring him up, Wolfe glanced down at the table and saw Jasper's face. He picked up the photograph. Jasper couldn't have been more than ten. He was holding a fishing pole with a fish dangling from the hook. Next to him stood a much younger-looking Uncle Jack. Like Wolfe, Jasper had lost both his parents. His mother had left when he was just a baby and his father had died in an oil rig accident when Jasper was twelve. But while Wolfe had his four siblings, Jasper only had his grandfather. And Uncle Jack had only had Jasper.

The photograph appeared to be covered with whiskey spots. But as Wolfe looked closer, he realized they weren't whiskey but tears.

He set the picture back on the table and got to his feet. While he had spent many a night carousing at the bar, he'd never been on the second floor. He'd never been invited. Not even when he and Jasper were kids. They'd always spent all their time out at the ranch. He didn't know what he expected to find, but it wasn't two small bedrooms and a tiny bathroom with moldy green tile.

No wonder Jasper had so much hatred inside. Wolfe had been living in a castle while his cousin had been living in abject poverty. He didn't understand it. Jasper had acted like the bar was doing so well. And Wolfe had witnessed it doing well. There were always people at the bar . . . until recently. Once the townsfolk had heard about Jasper, they had started to shun the bar. No one was dumb enough to be associated with someone who had pissed off the Kingmans. Wolfe had wanted the bar to close and his uncle to leave town and take all the memories with him.

But as he stood in the doorway of what must've been Jasper's room and stared at the small double bed with its tattered spread and the blacked-out window, he felt guilty as hell. Not just for wanting to punish Uncle Jack for what Jasper had done, but also for not knowing how grim their circumstances had been. For not doing anything to make them better. Maybe if he had, Jasper wouldn't have lost it and would be there right now with a smile and "Hey, cuz!"

With a hard knot of emotion lodged in his throat, he turned from the room and walked the short distance to the other bedroom. This one was slightly bigger with a window that actually let light in. Uncle Jack sat in an overstuffed chair looking out the window.

"Why are you still here, boy?"

It was a good question. One Wolfe didn't have an answer for. "I guess you'll need a new bartender if you want to keep the bar open."

Uncle Jack snorted. "You're a real genius. Now get gone."

Wolfe should have listened. It was obvious the ornery old cuss didn't want any company. But instead of leaving, he did something really stupid. "I bartended in college."

Uncle Jack turned to him and his shaggy white eyebrows lowered in confusion. "So? You want a medal, boy? And take your hat off in the house. Didn't any of your snobby relatives teach you manners?"

Wolfe pulled off his hat. "I can bartend for you. At least until you find someone else to do it."

Uncle Jack's eyes turned mean. "I'm not some charity case that needs a handout."

"I'm not talking about a handout. I'll expect to get paid."

"What are you up to? You think I'm stupid? Why would you want to work at a hole in the wall bar when you own one of the biggest ranches in Texas?"

Wolfe paused. "Because you're family. And you need help."

"I don't need shit. Especially from my black-hearted brother's kin."

"Yeah, you do. If you can't find a bartender, you'll go out of business."

"Maybe I'm ready to go out of business."

"Fine. I'll buy the bar from you." It would be the easiest way to assuage his conscience. Of course, he should've known his uncle wouldn't let it go that easy.

"The hell you will!" Uncle Jack snapped. "I'll never sell anything to your swindling family again."

"I'm only trying to help, you ornery old cuss."

Uncle Jack's eyes narrowed. "After what Jasper

did to your family, why would you want to help me?"

Wolfe shrugged. "You can't always judge a person by their family. I'm a perfect example. I'm about as far from my brother Stetson as a man can get." He grinned. "Besides, if the only bar in town goes out of business, I'll have to drive all the way to Amarillo to pick up women."

For a brief second, Wolfe thought he saw a smile tip the corners of his uncle's mouth. But if Jack had smiled, it was gone quickly. He grabbed a piece of junk mail from the pile sitting on the table next to the chair and started making a list on the back of the envelope. When he was finished, he held it out to Wolfe.

"Make them all and bring them to me. If you get them all right, I might think about hiring you. If you screw up just one, get your ass out of my bar and don't ever come back."

Wolfe looked at the envelope. It was a list of drinks. "Do you have a preference of brands? Because a cosmopolitan made with the house vodka tastes a lot different than a cosmopolitan made with Ketel One."

Uncle Jack snorted. "Just make the fuckin' drinks, smartass."

"Yes, sir." Wolfe turned and headed downstairs.

When he got behind the bar in the same place Jasper had always stood, his hands started to shake. What was he doing? Was he a glutton for punishment? It had been hard enough dealing with the memories of Jasper at the ranch. It would be impossible here. But then Uncle Jack came down the stairs and hollered, "I don't have all day, boy!" and Wolfe started making drinks.

The memories of Jasper faded.

In college, Wolfe had loved bartending. He'd always had a knack for multitasking and had enjoyed chatting up the customers. Especially the women. As he filled his uncle's orders, he quickly got back into the groove. He even spun a bottle of whiskey before pouring a shot in the glass. When he had all the drinks on a tray, he carried it to his uncle's table. Jack took his good sweet time tasting each drink before he pushed the tray away and looked at Wolfe.

"The margarita needed more salt on the rim. The Manhattan had two much vermouth. The martini should have one olive not two. And you forgot the triple sec in the Long Island iced tea."

As nitpicky as his uncle was being, Wolfe couldn't argue with his assessment of the drinks. He was impressed. The old guy knew his business. There was nothing left for Wolfe to do but keep his part of the bargain.

He picked up his cowboy hat. "Well, good luck, Uncle." He turned to leave, but Jack stopped him.

"Be here tomorrow an hour before we open. One minute late and don't bother coming in."

Wolfe grinned as he pulled on his hat. "Yes, sir."

It was funny. But as he headed out of the bar, he felt happier than he'd felt in a long time. He hadn't been able to help Jasper, but maybe he could help Jasper's grandfather. He had no desire to bartend forever. Just until the people of the town saw that not all the Kingmans were holding a grudge against Uncle Jack and started coming back to the bar. Once they did, Wolfe would find another bartender to take over. Or maybe he could convince his uncle to let him buy the bar.

Or maybe the ornery old cuss would fire him the first day out.

# Chapter Five

Gretchen and Adeline met every morning at ten o'clock in the sunroom off the kitchen for what they called a housekeeping meeting but was really a coffee klatch filled with plenty of giggles. They had only known each other for six months, but it felt like they had known each other for years. They talked about everything from the latest *Yellowstone* episode to town gossip. Today, the topic was what Hester Malone had said to Gretchen at church.

"You'll find true love in an unlikely place?" Adeline's blue eyes sparkled with excitement. "Maybe she was talking about church. You did say that the new pastor was kind of cute."

"He is cute, but Hester's prediction is wrong. I'm not looking for true love. My mama's search for her Mr. Right cured me of that." She had told Adeline all about her mama's multiple marriages . . . she just hadn't told her that one of her mama's husbands had been Adeline's daddy.

That was the dark secret Hester had been talking about.

Gretchen hadn't planned on keeping her

identity a secret. When she first came to Kingman Ranch, she had no plans to even meet her ex-step-siblings. She'd just wanted to see the fairytale castle her mother had told her about. But then Adeline had caught her sitting outside in her car and mistaken her for a housekeeping applicant. Since Gretchen had desperately wanted to see the inside of the castle, she'd gone along with the farce. The next thing she knew she was the Kingmans' new housekeeper and part of a big, boisterous household. A boisterous household that was everything an only child dreams about.

Stetson was the stern, protective big brother. His wife Lily the soft-spoken mediator. Adeline the kind-hearted big sister. Buck and Delaney the feuding younger siblings. And Wolfe the naughty bad boy with the charming smile.

The thought of the Kingmans finding out the truth made Gretchen physically ill. She knew it was wrong to lie to her best friend. But Delilah had kept Gretchen from having the security of a home as a child, and Gretchen refused to let her mama ruin her chance of a home as an adult. Delilah didn't even know she was here. She thought her only daughter was back in Little Rock working at a Kohl's.

"All I know is that if Hester thinks you're going to find true love, you will," Adeline said. "You just have to keep an open mind."

Before Gretchen could reply, Potts came walking into the room holding a pie plate. The crusty old cook looked fit to be tied.

"I don't know what in tarnation is going on,

but this is the second time I've found one of my pie plates in the trash."

Gretchen stared at the clear glass plate. The same one she had filled with a crust and apple pie filling the night before. Her peach pie had gone missing so she'd decided to make an apple pie for Wolfe. She'd woken up early to get the pie before someone else ate it. But just like the morning before, it was gone. From the looks of the scraped clean plate, the pie thief had enjoyed it.

"Who in the world would throw away pie plates?" Adeline asked.

"I'd say the person who baked and ate the pie."

She swallowed hard and confessed. "I baked the pies, but I didn't eat them. Or throw the plate in the trash. I don't know who did that. I'm sorry, Mr. Potts. I know you don't like people messing around in your kitchen."

"I don't like people gettin' in my way while I'm cooking," Potts said. "I don't mind people using the kitchen when I'm not around as long as they clean up after themselves. But you shouldn't be baking pies." He glanced at Adeline. "They bring up sad memories of Addie's mama."

Gretchen turned to Adeline. "Oh, Addie, I didn't know."

"Of course you didn't. How would you know that? It happened a long time ago. Everyone in the family got a little teary-eyed when Potts made pie right after mama passed and Daddy asked him not to make them anymore. But I think it's time to put pie back on the menu. If you like to bake, Gretchen, feel free to do so. I'm sure Potts would love not having to make dessert every night."

"I sure would," Potts said. "Of course, little good it will do if some gluttonous Kingman eats it all before anyone gets a slice." He looked at Adeline. "That doesn't include you, missy. You barely touched your omelet this morning. Don't tell me that you've gone back to picking at your food."

Adeline frowned. "I don't know what's the matter with me. Recently, just the thought of eggs makes me feel a little nauseated."

"Well, why didn't you say so sooner? I would've made French toast casserole this morning instead of omelets."

"I don't want you to have to change your menu for me, Potts. I'm sure it will pass."

Once Potts was gone, Gretchen turned to Adeline. "You didn't mention not feeling well."

"Because it's nothing. I've just felt a little queasy the last few mornings."

Gretchen studied her friend. "Could you be pregnant?"

Adeline shook her head. "Oh, no. My periods are always sporadic and Gage and I have been careful. Well . . . maybe not every time." She paused and her eyes widened. "Do you think I could be pregnant?"

"It's possible. Especially with you feeling sick just in the mornings."

"Pregnant." Adeline reverently touched her stomach. "Gage and I have talked about having kids, but we didn't plan on having them this soon. The thought of becoming a mother is kind of . . . terrifying." She glanced at Gretchen. "What if I'm horrible at it?"

Getting up from her chair, Gretchen joined Adeline on the loveseat and took her hands. "You won't be. From what I've heard, you were a great mom to Wolfe, Delaney, and Buck after your mama passed away. So you've got nothing to worry about. Now why don't you go find Gage and tell him about your suspicions? Then both of you head on into town and get a pregnancy test. Like my mama always says, 'No sense fretting about something until it comes to pass.'"

After Adeline left to find Gage, Gretchen headed to the laundry room to start a load of sheets. She was pouring detergent into the washing machine dispenser when a loud chiming startled her and caused her to spill the liquid detergent onto the floor. Since most the visitors to the house knocked on the kitchen door, it took another round of chimes before she recognized them as the doorbell.

Leaving the puddle of detergent on the floor, she hurried to answer it. She pulled open one of the massive front doors to find Reverend Ransom standing on the stoop.

Unlike Sunday, today he looked like a spit and polished pastor. His sandy hair was cut short and combed back, his handsome face was clean-shaven, and his western shirt was starched and as blue as the sky behind him. Even his speech seemed more formal.

"Good morning. I'm here to see Mr. Stetson Kingman."

"Well, hey, Reverend," Gretchen greeted him. "It's nice to see you again."

Reverend Ransom seemed confused. "Again?"

Figuring he'd met so many people on Sunday he'd forgotten her, she reintroduced herself. "I'm Gretchen Flaherty, the Kingman's housekeeper. We met on Sunday outside Holy Gospel."

A look of annoyance entered his eyes, but the emotion was gone so quickly Gretchen figured she was wrong. Why would the preacher be annoyed about their previous meeting? Unless Kitty had done something to tick him off. It was possible.

He nodded. "Of course. It's nice to see you again, Miss Flaherty."

"Just call me Gretchen."

"And you can call me Chance."

"Oh, I couldn't do that. My mama taught me to be respectful to preachers."

He smiled. He had a nice smile, if not a little hesitant—like he carried a great burden. And she figured he probably did. It had to be hard feeling responsible for people's souls. "As my grandmother always said, respect isn't in words as much as actions."

She laughed. "It sounds like my mama and your grandmother would have a lot to chat about." She held open the door. "Come on in, Chance. Stetson and his wife, Lily, aren't in town at the moment, but the rest of the family is. I'm sure one of them could help you with whatever you need."

He stepped into the foyer, and his eyes widened. "Wow."

"It does take some getting used to, doesn't it? When I first started working here, I got lost every day."

Chance continued to look around. "I can understand that. I grew up in a two-bedroom trailer the size of this foyer."

There was something endearing about a man who had come from humble beginnings and didn't mind talking about it. "A home is a home," Gretchen said. "No matter the size. Now come on into the sunroom. Adeline, Stetson's sister, should be back shortly and I know she'd love to meet you. I'll get you some coffee or sweet tea while you wait."

"Thank you, but I can't stay. I need to get back to Dallas. Reverend Floyd thought I should meet Mr. Kingman since I was just hired as Holy Gospel's new pastor."

"Congratulations! You must be excited."

Chance hesitated. "Yes."

His lack of enthusiasm had Gretchen lifting her eyebrows. "You don't sound very excited. Was there another pastoring position you were hoping for? I know small towns aren't for everyone."

"Actually, it has nothing to do with the town. Or another position. Just a personal matter that I had hoped to work out before I started pastoring again." The sadness in his eyes just about broke Gretchen's heart. She guessed everyone had their personal hardships to endure. Even preachers.

"Well, I'm sure glad you decided to take the position here in Cursed. If there's anything I can do to help you, you just let me know."

He paused. "Actually, there is something I need help with. Have you heard of the Cowboy Ball?"

"Is that a special football signed by the Dallas Cowboys?"

He laughed. "I wish it was that simple. I guess it's a dance that takes place every other spring in the church auxiliary gym and the ticket sales go to charity. The pastor's wife, Mrs. Floyd, was in charge of it. But since she'll be leaving with the pastor in a few months, she's stepping down and I need someone else to take over organizing the ball."

"I just moved here myself so I wouldn't be much help. But I know who would. Adeline. She plans all the celebrations here at the ranch—birthdays, weddings, and holidays. You couldn't get a better person to plan a ball. I'm sure she would be willing to do it."

"I hope so. I'm afraid planning and organizing parties isn't my strong suit."

"Well, you don't worry about the ball, Chance. If Adeline can't do it, I'll give it my best shot. But don't be surprised if you end up with more country hoedown than fancy ball."

Chance laughed. "Thank you, Gretchen. I can't tell you what a relief that is. How about if I call you when I get back into town and we can figure out the details?"

"What details?"

The deeply spoken words had Gretchen glancing up.

Wolfe stood at the top of the stairs. His hair was

messed and he wore nothing but a pair of faded jeans. To say he looked delicious with his hard, tattooed chest on display would be an understatement.

Ever since he'd driven her to church, Gretchen's mind had been conjuring up all kinds of wicked thoughts about Wolfe. Of course, truth be told, he had slipped into her fantasies long before Sunday. But that had been late at night when no one was around. Now those thoughts were showing up in the light of day. It was very disconcerting. Especially with the preacher standing right there.

She pulled her gaze away from his sexy wolf tattoo and pinned on a smile. "Good mornin'."

He moved down the stairs like a large cat stalking its prey. He stopped next to Gretchen—so close she could smell the soap she had used the night she had taken a bath in his tub. This time, a word didn't pop into her head. An image did. An image of Wolfe unzipping his jeans and . . .

Good Lord! What was she doing? She took a few steps away from him and spoke in a voice much higher than her normal range.

"This is Reverend Chance Ransom, Holy Gospel's new preacher. Chance, this is Wolfe Kingman, one of the owners of the Kingman Ranch."

The two men shook hands.

"It's a pleasure to meet you, Mr. Kingman," Chance said.

Wolfe nodded, but didn't reply. If his scowl was any indication, it looked like he had gotten up on the wrong side of the bed.

The pastor must have sensed it too because he quickly made his excuses.

"Well, I better be going." He pulled a business card from his shirt pocket and handed it to Gretchen. "This is my cellphone number. Call me any time. When I get back into town, we can hopefully meet up." He glanced at Wolfe. "I hope I'll see you in church, Mr. Kingman."

"Doubtful."

The pastor nodded. "Then maybe I'll see you around town." He smiled at Gretchen before he headed out the door.

When he was gone, Gretchen turned to Wolfe. "I know you don't particularly like church, but you could've been more cordial to the new pastor."

"Pastors shouldn't flirt."

"Flirt?" She laughed. "He wasn't flirting. He was just being nice." She slipped the pastor's card in the pocket of her apron and headed to the laundry room. She was surprised when Wolfe followed.

"Take my word for it, he was flirting. And why do you find that so unlikely?"

She turned to him. "Because I own a mirror."

His gaze swept her from head to toe. "Then maybe you need to buy another mirror."

A warm tingle spread through her. She didn't know if it was from Wolfe's heated gaze or his compliment. Of course, he probably complimented all women whether he found them attractive or not. That's what charming bad boys did.

Trying not to show him how his compliment had affected her, she turned and walked into the laundry room. Unfortunately, she forgot about the spilled detergent. Her feet hit the slippery puddle and flew out from under her. Wolfe tried to catch her, but his feet slipped in the soap too and they both went tumbling.

After the shock of falling wore off, Gretchen became aware of everything at once. She lay on top of Wolfe with his hard, naked chest beneath her head and his muscled arms encircling. As she listened to the steady thump of his heart, something hard grew against her lower stomach. When she realized what that something was, she felt completely stunned.

For a man who couldn't get it up, it felt pretty . . . up. What shocked her even more was that she was somehow responsible. Or maybe not. Maybe she had cracked her head when she fell and was lying on the floor unconscious. If that were the case, she might as well enjoy her unconscious fantasy.

She ran her hand over the hard muscles of his chest, cupping the pectoral with the snarling wolf tattoo. It looked so real. Vicious . . . but also kind of cute. She shifted and pressed her lips to the wolf's furry head. It growled. Or the real Wolfe growled. A deep, primitive sound that tugged at something deep inside of Gretchen.

She glanced up. Wolfe had lifted his head and was watching her with dark, heated eyes that matched his tattoo. She scooted up his body, until the part of her that ached brushed against his hard ridge. His lips parted. It was all the invitation she needed. She kissed him. She pressed her lips to his and slid her tongue into his hot mouth. He growled again and took over the kiss.

Although the word *kiss* didn't describe what he was doing to her. Kisses were sweet. There was nothing sweet about Wolfe's kiss. It was like he was a hungry predator, and she was his freshly-caught prey. His hot mouth consumed hers with wicked brushes of tongue and hungry nips of teeth. But his aggression didn't leave her feeling vulnerable. Instead, it made her feel desirable. Like she and only she could satisfy him.

Sliding her fingers through his thick hair, she gave him what he asked for, matching the hot slide of his lips and the wet thrust of his tongue. He tasted like apples and cinnamon. She couldn't get enough. She had just started to rub the needy pulse of her center against the hard throb of his fly when Buck's voice rang out.

"Anybody home?"

Wolfe pulled away. They stared at each other for a long moment before Wolfe lifted her off him and got to his feet. "Are you okay?" he asked as he helped her up.

All she could do was stare at his lips. Wow. No wonder women threw themselves at him. If he kissed like that, how would he make love?

He must've read her thoughts because he released a sigh and ran a hand through his hair. "Look, Gretchen, what just happened . . . shouldn't have happened. The preacher is a good choice for you. I'm not. Do you understand that?

I'm not for you."

His gaze lowered to her lips for one brief second before he turned and walked out.

When he was gone, Gretchen sagged back against the dryer and tried to collect herself. It took a while. Kissing Wolfe had been like riding a roller coaster after you'd only ever ridden merry-go-rounds. Kissing other men had been fun, but not even close to the heart-pounding thrill Wolfe had just given her. What was really depressing was that the ride was over. He'd pretty much told her it would never happen again.

She touched her lips. They still tingled.

But she hadn't thought it would happen at all.

And it had.

Who was to say that it wouldn't happen again?

## Chapter Six

"YOU REALLY LOVE to prod the bull, don't you, big brother?" Delaney said. "When Stetson finds out you're working as a bartender here, the shit is going to hit the fan."

Wolfe glanced at Delaney as he wiped down the bar. "And you can't wait to run home and tattle, can you?"

Delaney grinned. "What are little sisters for if not to tattle on their big brothers?" She sent him a wide-eyed innocent look. "But I might be persuaded to keep my mouth shut . . . for a price."

"And what would that be?"

"I want Mutt."

Wolfe laughed. "It figures you'd fall in love with that mangy horse."

"He's not mangy. He might not be much to look at, but I think he's got heart."

Wolfe had to agree. He'd spent the last few afternoons working with Mutt. He still wasn't tacking up and riding the horse, but he'd led him on walks and worked with him in the paddock with a long lead rope. Wolfe's online research hadn't pulled up any new information, but the horse did seem to have the quick reactions and instinct of a good cutting horse.

"Sorry, sis. I've gotten attached to Mutt."

Delaney looked confused. "But you're never gotten attached to one horse before."

It was true. Wolfe had never gotten attached to a particular horse. He gave each one the same amount of attention, choosing a different mount to ride each day. But Mutt was different. There was something about being around the horse that calmed Wolfe. He couldn't explain it. All he knew was that he needed calming right now.

He winked at his sister. "What can I say . . . maybe I'm getting more sentimental in my old age. And go ahead and tell Stetson that I'm working here. With the way this town loves to gossip about me, I'm surprised he hasn't heard already."

"I'm sure the townsfolk can't figure out why you would work for the grandfather of the man who caused so much trouble on the ranch. I can't figure it out either." Delaney glanced at Uncle Jack sitting at his table before she turned back to Wolfe. "All he's done since I've been here is yell at you. Why would you want to work for such an ornery old cuss? Especially when everyone in the family seems to think he was behind Jasper's vendetta."

Wolfe still didn't know for sure that his uncle hadn't been. But he couldn't desert the old dude. "If he was behind what happened out at the ranch, isn't it a good thing I'm here to keep an eye on him?" Not that he thought Uncle Jack could do anything to his family. He could barely get up and down the stairs.

Delaney studied him. "You can't fool me, bro. You might act tough, but you're just like me. You can't ignore a stray." She glanced around the bar. The only customers were two truckers playing pool. "But you helping bartend isn't going to save this place."

"Once the townsfolk see we aren't holding a grudge, they'll come back." At least, that's what he hoped. "You showing up here helps. Thanks, Del."

"It beats staying at home and dealing with our annoying little brother." She downed the last of her beer. "And speaking of town gossip, who's this new mystery woman you've lured into your bed?"

"Mystery woman?" He picked up her glass and refilled it from the tap—but only halfway. He didn't want her drinking too much and then driving home.

"No one seems to know her name. Which has Kitty Carson all in a tizzy and everyone in town trying to figure out who she is. The only person who claims they've seen her is Sue Ann Beck. She described her as a chubby redhead. Which is why the town has started calling her Red Riding Hood."

The glass slipped from his hand and crashed to the floor, splashing beer everywhere.

"That will come out of your paycheck, boy!" Uncle Jack yelled.

Wolfe didn't acknowledge his uncle as he stared at Delaney. "Red Riding Hood?"

Delaney's blue eyes twinkled. "Don't you get

it? She's got red hair and you're the big bad wolf. But the entire chubby thing has me puzzled. I've never seen you date an overweight woman."

"She's not overweight." After having her body pressed against his, he could attest to that fact. Gretchen wasn't fat. She was curvaceous, shapely, voluptuous . . . and perfect. Just not perfect for him. He thanked his lucky stars Buck had shown up when he did.

Wolfe had kissed a lot of women in his life, but not one had ever kissed him like Gretchen. The women he dated didn't like to waste a lot of time on kissing. They wanted to get straight to sexual satisfaction. Their sexual satisfaction. But Gretchen seemed satisfied just being in his arms and kissing. The weird part about it was he hadn't been in any hurry to get to the sex part either. Even when his cock had been begging for release. And that scared him. Scared him more than he was willing to admit.

He bent down and started cleaning up the broken glass.

Delaney peeked over the bar, her braids swinging. "I figured Sue Ann was just being a petty bitch. She hates anyone who gets your attention. So who is your new girlfriend?"

"Gretchen's not my girlfriend." He tossed the broken glass in the trash bin.

"Gretchen? Our Gretchen? You're fooling around with the housekeeper?"

"Would you lower your voice?" Wolfe got to his feet and glanced at the truckers. They had stopped playing pool and were looking over. But, luckily, they weren't from around there. "I'll bring you a couple more beers," he said. The truckers nodded and went back to their game.

As he started to fill a glass, Delaney spoke in a slightly lower voice. "Have you lost your mind, Wolfe? If you think Stetson is going to be mad about you working for Uncle Jack, it will be nothing compared to how pissed Adeline will get when she finds out you're screwing her new best friend."

"I'm not screwing Gretchen." Or kissing her again. He didn't seduce sweet country girls ... no matter how much they set him on fire.

"So why was she naked in your bathtub?" Delaney asked.

"Sue Ann said Gretchen was naked in my tub?" It figured Sue Ann would share all the details. He finished filling the glass and started filling another. "It was all a misunderstanding. Gretchen's faucet broke in her bathroom so she used my bathtub because I was out of town. But I came back early and Sue Ann saw me at the gas station and decided to follow me home. When she discovered Gretchen in my tub, she jumped to the wrong conclusion."

Or maybe not jumped. He'd led her to the wrong conclusion. All because he didn't want her finding out he couldn't get an erection. His ego hadn't thought about the backlash. Delaney was happy to point it out.

"Well, it doesn't matter if it's the wrong conclusion or not. Once folks find out who the redhead was in your bathtub, gossip is going to fly about you having an affair with our housekeeper."

He blew out his breath. "Shit."

"I'd say you were knee deep in it, big bro. But it's Gretchen who will get the brunt of it."

Delaney was right. The townsfolk expected him to be bad. And being a Kingman, most of his sins were easily forgiven. But Gretchen wasn't a Kingman. She wasn't even considered a resident of the town. A person needed to live in Cursed for a good ten years before folks thought of them as local. Gretchen was still an outsider. And outsiders were harshly judged.

Wolfe ran a hand over the scruff of his beard. "So how do I fix this?"

"Beats the hell out of me. My boring life has never been gossip worthy. If someone thought I was having a torrid affair with a bad boy, I wouldn't be upset. I'd be strutting around town like a peacock."

"Because you don't give a damn what people think."

She grinned. "And don't you know it, big bro. But Gretchen cares a lot about people liking her. That's why she works so hard to get you to."

"She's works hard? All she's done is attack me." And turn him on.

Delaney laughed. "And here I thought my big brother knew everything about women. She's just gets nervous around you. Probably because she thinks you're hot."

Gretchen thinking he was hot was the last thing he wanted to hear. Probably because he thought she was hot too. Which wasn't a good thing.

He'd prefer to still be annoyed with her. But he wasn't annoyed any more. He was becoming . . . obsessed. He needed to get un-obsessed. Besides not being his type, she was Adeline's friend and their housekeeper. Screwing with her was a bad idea. It wouldn't just piss off Adeline. It would also piss off Stetson. Wolfe needed to make sure neither one of his siblings found out about the kiss . . . or the bathtub incident.

He thought for a moment before he looked at his sister. "Nobody knows who Red Riding Hood is, right?"

"As far as I can tell."

"So all we have to do is make sure that nobody figures it out. Which should be easy since Sue Ann is the only one who saw her. And Sue Ann is headed to Dallas in a couple weeks to take that new job her sister got her. If you can keep Gretchen from coming into town and running into Sue Ann for the next couple weeks, no one will be the wiser."

Delaney tipped her head. "If I can keep Gretchen from coming into town?"

"Come on, Del," he pleaded. "Help me out here. I can't keep Gretchen from coming into town while I'm working here. And you don't want her getting hurt by ugly gossip, do you? Or your favorite brother getting killed by Adeline?"

She scrunched up her eyes in thought. "I don't know about that. One less brother to make my life a living hell sounds kinda nice." Wolfe sent her his best puppy dog look, and she laughed. "Fine, I'll help you. But only at night when you're working. You'll be responsible for keeping her at the ranch during the day. In return for my help, I want to train Mutt."

Since his little sister was one of the best horse trainers in Texas, he figured he was getting a great bargain. "Deal." He reached out and tugged one of her braids. "You've always been my favorite baby sister."

"I'm your only baby sister."

"Just details."

She rolled her eyes as she slid off the barstool. "Now if you will excuse me, I'm going to go play pool with those two truckers. If I can't get a man in bed, I can at least take all their money."

Wolfe laughed. "Go easy on them, Del. We need to keep customers, not run them off."

When she was gone, he took the beer to the truckers and then went into the kitchen to get a mop to clean up the floor. The kitchen had everything. A commercial cooktop, double ovens, a fryer, and a walk-in refrigerator. With a kitchen like this, the bar could easily serve food. And yet, Wolfe couldn't remember his uncle serving anything but tacos on Tuesdays. It had been the busiest night of the week for the bar.

"What the hell are you doing in here, boy? Are you smoking that loco weed?"

Wolfe glanced at the doorway to see his uncle standing there scowling. "I'm not smoking loco weed. I was getting a mop to clean up the beer I spilled. Why did you only serve food on Tuesday nights?"

"It was the only night Otis was willing to work.

Now quit messing around and get back to the bar."

"In case you haven't noticed, we only have two customers. And I already got them beers. Otis Davenport? He cooked for you on Tuesdays?" Otis owned the Good Eats restaurant in town with his wife, Thelma.

"You know another Otis in town?" his uncle snapped.

"Why did he quit?"

"How the hell would I know? Now quit standing here asking me stupid questions and get back to the bar."

Wolfe followed his uncle out of the kitchen, but he couldn't stop thinking about Taco Tuesdays. People could stock up on beer and alcohol, but getting take out food wasn't so easy in a small town. Good Eats was only open for breakfast and lunch because Otis and Thelma liked to spend time with their numerous kids and grandkids. Which meant that there was no place to eat dinner out in Cursed. The crowd that showed up for Taco Tuesdays proved the townsfolk liked to eat out. If Wolfe could talk Otis into coming back and cooking for them a couple times a week, maybe he could keep the bar from going under.

As Wolfe finished mopping, the door opened and a cowboy walked in. The brim of his cowboy hat shadowed most of his face, but there was something about his mouth that looked vaguely familiar as he ordered a bottle of Coors.

"You from around here?" Wolfe asked as he opened the bottle and set it on the bar.

"Nope. Just passing through." He pulled out a crumpled ten from his pocket. "Keep the change." Then he picked up his beer and headed to the pool tables.

Wolfe watched as the man respectfully tipped his hat at Delaney, and then took a seat to wait for his turn to play the winner. Wolfe didn't doubt for a second that it would be his sister. He watched for a few minutes more before he finished mopping and took the mop back to the kitchen. While he was there, he checked out the stove and cooktop to make sure they were in working order. Then he looked in the refrigerator. Some of the food needed to be thrown out, but there was some that hadn't expired, including the boxes of ground beef and chicken in the freezer. He tossed a couple packages of moldy cheese before he headed back out to the bar.

When he got there, he discovered that both the cowboy and Delaney were gone.

Shit.

He headed over to the truckers who were still playing pool. "Where's the woman who was playing with you?"

The trucker with the thick mustache spoke. "She followed that cowboy out the door awhile back."

Wolfe hurried for the door, praying he would catch his sister before she did something stupid. As soon as he pulled the door open, he stopped short. Uncle Jack stood in the parking lot pointing a gun at the cowboy who had both hands in the air.

"I swear I wasn't doing anything but kissing her, sir. And she was more than willing. In fact, she was the one who followed me out to my truck."

"I don't give a shit who did what." Uncle Jack waved the gun. "You get your ass off my property and don't come back. I won't have any hanky panky at my bar."

The cowboy nodded. "Yes, sir." He tipped his hat at Delaney before he got in his beat up truck and took off.

Delaney yelled after him. "Wait! You have my boot." Sure enough, it looked like she was wearing only one boot. Wolfe was thankful that was all she'd lost. Although it looked like she had lost her temper too. She whirled on Uncle Jack. "Are you kidding me? You can't just go around waving guns at people."

Uncle Jack lowered the gun. "I can if it's my bar."

Delaney stomped her one boot. "Urghhh! I've had it up to my neck with the double standards in my family! Wolfe and Buck can run around town like horny bulls, but because I'm a woman I'm supposed to act like a sweet little virgin. Well, I'm not sweet and I'm sick to death of being a virgin."

"Me coming out here had nothing to do with you being a girl, little girl," Uncle Jack said. "It had to do with that man being a stranger. You want to act like a horny bull, you go ahead and act like a horny bull. But you do it with people you know and trust. You don't do it with some drifter who just walked in off the street and could slit your throat before anyone knew you were gone."

Delaney's anger seemed to fizzle, and she released a long sigh. "Fine. I guess I shouldn't have hopped in a truck with a man I didn't know. But all the men I know are too afraid of my brothers to mess around with me."

"Then you haven't found the right man. When you do, he won't care how big and mean your brothers are. All he'll care about is being with you. Now get on inside before Wolfe discovers you're gone."

Wolfe quickly closed the door before Uncle Jack or Delaney could see him. He went back to the kitchen and waited a few minutes before he came back out. Delaney was sitting at the bar scowling and Uncle Jack was sitting at the table.

When he saw Wolfe, he yelled, "Don't just stand there looking stupid, boy. Get that bar polished. I can see a smudge."

Wolfe grinned. "Yes, sir."

## Chapter Seven

"Why wouldn't the new pastor be interested in you? You're a beautiful woman."

Gretchen smiled at Adeline's compliment. "Thanks, Addie, but I think you're looking through rose-tinted glasses. I'm no beauty. My hair is too curly. My face is too freckled. And my body is too . . . much."

"Your curly hair is gorgeous," Adeline said. "You just need to stop confining it. The only freckles you have are across your nose and cheeks. And you're not too much. You're curvy. I wish I had the curves you've got."

"No one wants a curvy stomach."

Adeline placed a hand on her stomach and smiled. "I do."

Gretchen couldn't help releasing a little squeal of joy. "I'm so happy for you, Addie." She glanced around the sunroom. On every flat surface there was a bouquet of beautiful flowers. "And it looks like Gage is positively thrilled. Although if he keeps sending you flowers, you're going to have to add a room to the castle."

Adeline laughed. "I told him that he had to stop." Her eyes turned all misty. "He said he'd never stop filling my life with flowers."

Gretchen sighed. "You got yourself a good man, Mrs. Reardon."

"I do. And I want you to get yourself one too." Adeline picked up Gretchen's cell phone from the table. "Chance said to call him anytime. So call him. You can tell him you're calling to let him know that you talked with me and I'd be happy to take over the Cowboy Ball. In fact, I plan to bring it up at the Cursed Ladies' Auxiliary meeting this morning. I'm sure all the women will be happy to help too." Her eyes lit up. "Why don't you come with me? You should join the club."

"Oh, I don't know, Addie. That's an exclusive club. Only the most important women of Cursed belong to it."

Adeline laughed. "Those are Kitty Carson's words if ever I've heard them. The Cursed Ladies' Auxiliary club is just a bunch of ordinary women who love to get together and gossip under the guise of raising money for the town."

"Still, I'm not really part of the town. The townsfolk have been friendly, but in the same hesitant way you're friendly to a stranger who shows up at your door uninvited."

"It just takes a little while for folks to warm up. But what better way to help them warm up than to join the club." Adeline sent Gretchen a pointed look. "And if the ladies decide to take on the Cowboy Ball, we'll need a liaison to get all our plans okayed by the cute new pastor." She held out the phone. "Now call him."

Gretchen hesitated for only a second before she took the phone. "Did anyone ever tell you that you're as stubborn as a starving dog with a bone?"

"Only Gage and my entire family." Adeline got up. "Now I'm going to go finish packing." Adeline and Gage were leaving for Gage's family ranch right after Adeline got back from the ladies' meeting. They wanted to tell Gage's family in person the news about Adeline being pregnant.

When she was gone, Gretchen pulled the card Pastor Chance had given her out of her apron pocket and tapped in his number. She was hoping she could just leave a message, but he answered. He seemed happy to hear from her and even happier Adeline was going to help with the Cowboy Ball.

"That's wonderful news! I can't thank you enough."

"Oh, it wasn't me. Addie is just a good person."

"I'm sure she is, but you helped convince her." He paused. "I hope you still plan to help too."

"I guess I'm going to be the liaison between you and the women's club."

"Excellent! How about we have dinner when I get back into town and we can discuss their plans then?"

*Dinner?* Obviously, Adeline was right. The pastor was interested in her. Gretchen should be thrilled she'd caught the attention of such an attractive man. Unfortunately, Wolfe had set the thrill bar way too high. A dinner invitation didn't compare to a hungry kiss on a laundry room floor. That was just wrong. All wrong. She had no business mooning over Wolfe. She had just secured her place in the Kingman household. And she wasn't about to ruin it by becoming obsessed with a man who had probably kissed hundreds of women.

"I'd love to go to dinner with you," she said.

"Perfect. I'll call you when I get back in town."

"Talk to you then." After hanging up, she stood and turned to head into the kitchen. She stopped short when she saw Wolfe lounging in the doorway with his shoulder propped on the doorframe.

She hadn't seen him since the kiss. He had started sleeping late—probably because he was out carousing until all hours of the night—then left the house for the stables as soon as he woke up. He looked like he was headed for the stables today. He wore a black t-shirt that hugged his biceps, faded wranglers, scuffed boots, and the stained straw cowboy hat he always wore around the ranch. Beneath the shadow of the brim, his gray eyes were piercing . . . and heart stopping.

"Sounds like you have a date."

She didn't know why she blushed. "It's not really a date. We're just meeting to plan the Cowboy Ball."

He tipped his head. "Why do you do that?"

"Do what?"

"Act like you're not worthy of a man's attention. If he just wanted to talk about the Cowboy Ball, he could do that over the phone. He's interested in you." His smoky gaze lowered to her mouth.

Just like that, she couldn't seem to draw enough oxygen into her lungs to feed her brain. Thankfully, before she could do something really stupid like pass out—or dive into his arms—Adeline showed up.

"Good morning, little brother. I'm surprised you're up so early after the late nights you've been keeping." Adeline hooked her arm through his and gave him a sassy smile. "Your late nights wouldn't have anything to do with the redhead everyone in town is talking about, would they?"

A redhead? Wolfe was seeing a redhead? Gretchen didn't know why she felt so hurt. She knew he'd been out carousing. She just thought it was with different women. She hadn't thought it was with one particular woman. The thought made Gretchen realize what an idiot she was being. What difference did it make if Wolfe dated one woman or a million? She needed to stop acting like a ninny over one little ol' kiss and move on.

"You're dating a redhead?" She winked at Wolfe. "You better be careful. Us redheads have been known to have hot tempers."

Adeline laughed, but Wolfe didn't seem to find it amusing. In fact, he didn't look happy at all.

"We're not dating," he growled.

"Well, maybe it's time you started," Adeline said "In fact, why don't you invite this redhead to dinner some night. But wait until Gage and I get back from Sagebrush Ranch."

"How long will you be gone?" Wolfe asked.

"A couple weeks. So try and help Stetson as

much as you can."

Wolfe snorted. "Our big brother doesn't need any help from me. He's made that more than clear."

"Then just try to get along with him while I'm gone and keep Buck and Delaney from killing each other." Adeline glanced over at Gretchen. "Come on, Gretchen. Let's head into town so we can stop by Good Eats and grab a couple of Otis's donuts before the ladies'—"

Wolfe cut her off. "Gretchen can't go into town."

Adeline turned to him. "Why not?"

"Because . . . I have something I need her to do for me."

Since Gretchen didn't want to barge in on the ladies' club meeting anyway, she latched onto the excuse. "You go ahead without me, Addie. If Wolfe needs my help with something, I'm happy to stay and help him. That's my job. I'll go to a meeting with you another time."

Adeline hesitated for a second before she nodded. "Fine. But you're coming with me next time. I don't care how exclusive Kitty thinks our club is."

After Adeline left, Gretchen turned to Wolfe. He still looked handsome as sin lounging in the doorway. It was still difficult to keep her gaze off his mouth. But finding out about his redhead had given her the reality check she'd needed. He had been right. He wasn't for her.

"What did you need?" she asked.

He stood there for a long time, like he was having trouble finding the words. Then his stomach growled loudly. "Food," he said. "I'm starving and Potts left for the grocery store. I was hoping you know how to cook."

She smiled. "I think I can whip you up something."

When she got to the kitchen and started cooking, it was like stepping into her favorite pair of flannel pajamas. She immediately felt comfortable, relaxed, and as happy as a pig in mud.

Which probably explained why she went a little overboard.

She didn't just make her mama's stuffed French toast with cinnamon cream cheese filling and fresh peach topping. She also made oven-baked bacon in brown sugar and maple syrup and fried potatoes with onion and jalapenos. When everything was finished, she filled a plate to overflowing and turned to the table. But Wolfe wasn't sitting at the table. He had moved to the island and was staring at her in stunned shock.

"Where did you learn to cook like that?"

She set the plate in front of him and made a plate for herself. Because what's the fun of cooking if you can't taste the finished product?

"My mama," she said as she took a barstool a good ways away from Wolfe. She had put their kiss behind her, but she still didn't want to test fate. "She's an awesome cook, which is how she landed so many husbands. 'The best way to a man's heart is through his stomach.' Her specialty is pies. She made pies whenever we moved to a new town. Her pies were what helped her make new friends in the neighborhood. No one can resist pie."

He flashed a smile. "So you're the one who made the delicious pies."

She stared at him. "You tasted my pies?"

He nodded and held a finger to his lips. "But don't tell Potts. I convinced him it was Buck who threw his pie plate in the trash."

She laughed. "Isn't that just life for you? I made the pies for you and you turned out to be the pie thief."

"You made the pies for me?"

"I thought if it made the neighbors like my mama, it would help you like me."

He studied her for a long moment before he spoke. "I like you, Gretchen."

She couldn't describe the feeling that bloomed inside her. Her heart started thumping overtime against her ribcage and her palms got all sweaty. The kiss popped into her head, but she shoved it right back out again. Being friends with Wolfe was much better than kissing him. At least, that's what she planned to keep telling herself.

"See." She grinned. "No one can resist pie."

He flashed another smile before he picked up his fork and took a big bite of the French toast and peaches.

She didn't know why watching Wolfe enjoy her cooking made her feel so happy and proud. Every yummy noise he made stroked her ego . . . and made her feel all breathless and overheated.

After he'd helped himself to seconds, he glanced at her. "Why are you a housekeeper and not a chef?"

Since she couldn't tell him that her getting the job as a housekeeper had all been a mistake, she only shrugged. "I like cleaning house too."

"But it's obvious that you love cooking. If you love doing something, you should do it." He picked up a piece of bacon and took a bite, closing his eyes in ecstasy. "Especially if you're good at it. Talents should not be ignored. Not all us of have them."

His words surprised her. "You have talents."

He laughed. "I don't know if I'd call chasing women and carousing a talent."

"I'm not talking about that. I'm talking about ranching. Few people could run a ranch this big."

He stopped eating and stared out the window. "I don't run this ranch. Stetson does."

"But you help him."

"Not much. Stetson runs the ranch. Adeline runs the house. Delaney works with the horses . . . and her goats. Buck is in charge of the cattle. And I'm just the odd man out who's more trouble than I'm worth."

She stared at him. "That's not true. You help on the ranch. You're traveling all the time and buying livestock."

"And not doing it particularly well. I guess you haven't heard about Mutt."

"Mutt? Is that a dog?"

"No, he's a horse." He hesitated for only a second before he pushed back from the bar and stood. "Come on, I'll show you."

"Oh, I couldn't. I need to clean up the dishes

before Potts gets back."

"I'll help clean up." Wolfe's gaze swept over her. "But first, we need to find you some jeans and riding boots, Red."

## Chapter Eight

Wolfe made a big mistake talking Gretchen into changing out of her dress and apron and into a t-shirt and jeans. When she stepped back into the kitchen a few minutes later, he almost choked to death on the last bite of bacon he'd put in his mouth. He had never seen her in anything but loose dresses that hit her well below the knees. Seeing her in tight jeans and a soft cotton t-shirt was like seeing a sheep without its wool. There was nothing to hide the body beneath.

Gretchen had one damn fine body.

The full curves of her top matched the full curves of her bottom in a perfect hourglass shape. All that delightful flesh seemed to jiggle and wiggle as she hurried over to smack him on the back to get him to stop choking.

In the process, she knocked over the open container of juice sitting on the counter and spilled it all over him. Which was probably a good thing. He needed cooling down and a reminder that Gretchen wasn't for him . . . no matter how hot she looked in a pair of Levi's.

"Oh, no!" She grabbed a dishtowel and went for his wet crotch, but he took the towel from her. The last thing he needed was Gretchen touching him there.

"I'm fine. I'll just go change."

After he changed clothes, he stopped by Delaney's room and grabbed a pair of her cowboy boots from her closet. When he got to the kitchen, he found Gretchen washing the dishes. Trying to keep his mind off how fine her ass looked in the jeans, he helped her dry the last few pans and put them away before he handed her the boots.

"See if these fit."

She sat down in one of the kitchen chairs to put them on. But it was obvious she hadn't worn cowboy boots before by the way she was trying to cram her foot in.

"I think they're too small."

Wolfe knelt and took the boot from her. "Cowboy boots are made to fit snug so they take a little more effort to get on." He lifted her foot and pressed her toes into a point before guiding it into the shank of the boot. Then he grabbed the pull loops at the top and gave a firm tug. When her foot was in, he leaned back.

"How does it feel? Snug but not too snug?"

She nodded. "They fit like a glove. I guess my mama was right. Sometimes getting the perfect fit just takes a little work."

He laughed as he stood. "Does your mama have a saying for everything?"

"Pretty much. Although she rarely follows her own advice. Which is why she's had six husbands."

"Six?" He helped her to her feet. She had the softest hands and he held onto them a little longer than he should have before he released her.

"Mama says seven is going to be her lucky number. But that's doubtful. Love doesn't have anything to do with luck. It has to do with unselfishness, dedication, and hard work. Three traits my mama doesn't have."

Wolfe held open the back door. "I don't have them either. Which is why I have no intentions of getting married."

Gretchen gave him a thoughtful look on her way past. "You know I used to think you were cocky. I didn't realize you have low self-esteem."

Her words took him by surprise. "I don't have low self-esteem," he said as they headed to the stables.

"I don't know what else you'd call thinking you're a selfish, undedicated, lazy spare part."

Since he had just said those exact things, he couldn't deny it. Maybe that's why he acted so cocky. He was trying to hide the insecure man beneath.

"And what about you?" He glanced over at her. "I wouldn't exactly say you have a high opinion of yourself."

She nodded. "You're right. Maybe we both need to think a little more highly of ourselves. As my mama always says, 'Nobody is gonna love you if you can't love yourself.'"

Wolfe couldn't help but smile as he led her through the open doors of the stable.

As soon as they entered, Gretchen gasped. "It's

beautiful."

Having spent so much time in the stables, he'd forgotten how impressive they were. Inside was long row of stalls made of all natural wood stained a dark finish. The doors on the opposite end were open wide and afternoon sunlight poured in, lighting the particles in the air and making it look like Lily's fairies were sprinkling their magic dust down from the big-beamed rafters.

In the midst of the fairy dust was Gretchen with her golden red hair and her sparkling green eyes that held wonder and awe. Wolfe couldn't remember the last time he'd felt wonder and awe. But he felt like he was experiencing it now through Gretchen.

"I'm assuming you haven't been out here before," he said.

She shook her head. "I'm pretty busy in the house."

"You're not that busy. I know my sister would give you time off whenever you wanted."

"Addie would, but I don't think I should be nosing around the ranch."

"It's your home, too, Gretchen. You're welcome to go anywhere you want to."

The startled look she gave him made him realize just how unwelcoming he'd been to her. He felt bad about that. When she'd first arrived, he'd thought she had something against him and was purposely trying to make his life hell. But he realized now that all the spills, intrusions, and fire hadn't been intentional. Gretchen didn't have a mean bone in her body. His gaze swept over her.

Just lots of sweet, soft curves.

"Except your room."

Her words pulled his gaze back to her face. "Excuse me?"

"I'm not welcome in your room." He could tell by her impish smile she was teasing him, but there was nothing funny about the image that popped into his head of her tangled in his sheets.

"Come on," he said. "This way."

When Gretchen saw Mutt, she reacted like everyone else did. Stunned and speechless.

"He's . . . umm . . ."

Wolfe laughed. "I know. He's not much to look at, but he's a sweet guy." To prove it, as soon as they stepped into the stall, Mutt came over to greet them. He nuzzled Wolfe first before he did the same to Gretchen.

She giggled. "You're right. He is sweet. But I guess Stetson wasn't looking for you to bring home sweet from the auction."

"I didn't buy him at the auction. I won him in a poker game." He knelt and checked the horse's forelocks. The tendons were no longer swollen. It was time to see how well the horse did with a rider. He stood. "You ride, Red?" The nickname just seemed to pop out of his mouth. He blamed Delaney for putting Red Riding Hood into his head.

"I rode a little as a kid. I don't know if I remember any of it."

"Riding a horse is like riding a bike. You never forget."

But as he saddled one of the more gentle

mounts for Gretchen, he started to worry. She wasn't exactly an agile woman. What if she fell off the horse and broke her neck?

He was about to make up an excuse for why they couldn't ride when Gretchen hooked her foot in the stirrup and tossed her leg over the horse like a pro. Of course, watching her curvy butt adjust to the saddle made the first few minutes of their ride extremely uncomfortable for Wolfe. Thankfully, Mutt helped him refocus.

Wolfe put the horse through his paces—taking him from a walk to a trot and then back to a walk. The horse was well-trained and followed Wolfe's direction with just a slight shift of body weight and leg pressure.

Surprisingly, Gretchen had no trouble keeping up. After they'd ridden for a while, he slowed Mutt to a walk and glanced over at her.

"Who taught you to ride?"

"My daddy."

"What number was he?"

"Two. He's a rodeo announcer. He wanted to be a bronc rider, but he wasn't good enough. He hoped his child would be." She shrugged and smiled. "But I popped out a clumsy girl and ruined his dreams of having a son who's a rodeo star. He still couldn't have a kid who didn't know how to ride. It was the one thing he made sure I knew before he and mama divorced." She kept the smile in place, but her eyes held sadness. Wolfe understood that sadness.

"Do you see him?" he asked.

"Not much. But I talk to him . . . occasionally.

We don't really know what to say to each other."

Wolfe nodded as he guided Mutt around a gopher hole. "My daddy and I didn't have much to say to each other either. Which is weird since we were two peas in a pod."

"How so?"

"My daddy loved women as much as I do. That was how he broke my mama's heart."

"So that's why you don't want to get married. You don't want to break a woman's heart like your daddy did your mama's."

It shocked him that Gretchen had read him so easily. Especially when no one else ever had. He glanced over to see her looking at him with clear green eyes that sparkled with tears.

"Adeline told me how beautiful your mama was," she said. "And what a good horsewoman. I'm sorry you lost her so young."

Wolfe had never liked sympathy. Especially from a woman. But there was something about Gretchen's that didn't make him feel weak. It made him feel . . . better.

"I don't really remember her," he said. "I want to. But there's nothing there. I was only seven when she died. Stetson is the keeper of all the Mom memories. He used to tell us stories about her every night."

"What was your favorite?"

He thought for a moment before he answered. "When I was three, she put me on my first horse. I guess I must've liked it because every time she went to take me off, I started bawling my eyes out. So she led me around the paddock all afternoon until I finally fell asleep right over the saddle horn."

"She sounds like a good mama."

"Yeah. She deserved a better man than my daddy."

"Maybe she didn't think so. Maybe, for all his faults, she still loved him."

A lump formed in Wolfe's throat and a burning sensation pushed at the back of his eyes. Before he embarrassed himself, he needed to get away from Gretchen.

"I think I'll let Mutt stretch his legs." He put his heels to Mutt, and the horse took off. He seemed to sense Wolfe's need for speed and ran like the wind. Hell, he could place in a horserace he ran so fast. Then, out of nowhere, he put on the brakes and almost tossed Wolfe right over his neck. Wolfe had just gotten his seat back when the horse whirled to a cluster of mesquite bushes. The rustling alerted Wolfe that there was something inside just as Mutt started to lunge first one way and then the other.

Wolfe had seen a lot of cutting horses, but he'd never seen one move as quickly as Mutt did. Or so low to the ground. Suddenly, out from the mesquite bush came a little Angus calf. The cow and horse played a game of tag. The calf dodged one way and then the other, trying to get around the horse and to open range. But Mutt's quick movements kept him pinned against the mesquite bushes. Until the calf grew tried and just stopped.

Mutt stood over the cow like a sentinel, his

chest heaving, his fly-bitten ears flicking, and his breath huffing from his nostrils. After only a stunned moment, Wolfe tipped back his head and laughed at the blue Texas sky.

"What happened?" Gretchen came riding up. "What's so funny?"

Wolfe grinned at her. "It seems that Mutt is a prize worth winning after all."

But he never got a chance to prove it to his brother.

When they got back to the ranch, Stetson was waiting outside the stables. Wolfe started to tell him about Mutt and rub his nose in it a little, but his brother cut him off.

"We need to talk."

"You know I'm always happy to talk, Stet," Wolfe said as he dismounted. He handed the reins to Tab, who was waiting for them with an uneasy look on his face, then went to help Gretchen dismount.

Once on the ground, she was smart enough to make a quick exit. "If you'll pardon me. I need to get back to the house." But before she hurried away, she did the strangest thing. She placed a hand on Wolfe's forearm and gave it a reassuring squeeze. There was nothing sexual about it, and yet, it filled him with such longing he couldn't take his eyes off her as she walked away.

"You better not be thinking what I think you're thinking."

Wolfe turned to see Stetson glaring at him.

"She works for us, Wolfe. And you'll damn well respect her. I won't have you seducing her by taking her on afternoon rides."

"I wasn't seducing her. She'd never been to the stables and I was just showing her around." And keeping her from going into town and being recognized by Sue Ann. But he couldn't tell his brother about that. Not when he already looked so pissed.

"What the hell is wrong with you?" Stetson snapped. "You've tried my patience before, but lately, you've been doing everything you can to tick me off. First, you buy that piece of shit horse." He waved a hand at Mutt who was being led into the stables by Tab. "Then I find out that you've started bartending at Nasty Jack's without saying a word to me. And now you're chasing after our housekeeper and Adeline's good friend. Are you trying to get your ass kicked off this ranch?"

"You can't kick me off my own ranch, Stet."

"The hell I can't. You might own a piece of the business, but Daddy put the house in my name and my name only."

Wolfe stared at him. "So you're kicking me out of the house?"

"Only if you can't get your act together. Stay away from Gretchen and quit working at Nasty Jack's. I refuse to have you working for the man who was behind Lily being attacked and Adeline almost getting killed."

"There's no proof that Uncle Jack had anything to do with Jasper's crimes."

Stetson stared at him. "The hell he didn't. Jack has hated our family ever since King bought him out."

"More like swindled him."

Stetson stared at him. "Now you're siding with Jack and think he was swindled out of this land?"

Wolfe had never given his family's history much thought until Uncle Jack had pointed it out. Lately, he couldn't stop thinking about the reason behind Jasper's need for vengeance. And Jack's hatred of his brother's family.

"What if Uncle Jack is right, Stet? What if King did swindle his brother out of this ranch? You told me yourself how ruthless our grandfather was. King would do whatever it took to get more land and make more money—even at the cost of his family's happiness." He paused. "Did King convince Daddy to marry Mama to get her land?"

"Jack told you that?"

Wolfe nodded. "Is it true?" Stetson's silence was answer enough. "Why didn't you tell me?"

"Because I didn't think it was something you needed to know."

Wolfe exploded. "That is such bullshit! They were my parents too, Stet."

"Which is why I didn't want you to know. I didn't want my siblings having to live with the fact that our parents didn't love each other. At least, Daddy didn't love Mama."

Wolfe felt like he'd been hit in the gut. Deep down he'd wanted to believe Uncle Jack had been lying. He knew his father was a womanizer, but he'd thought he'd loved his mother. Now he realized that he hadn't loved her at all. Maybe men like him and his father couldn't love that deeply.

He turned to Stetson. "If King talked Daddy into marrying a woman he didn't love just so he could get his hands on Mama's land. I'd say it's extremely possible King swindled his own brother."

"So you're saying Jasper had a right to do what he did?"

"No, I'm not saying that at all. I'm saying that maybe we do owe them something."

"I offered Uncle Jack something," Stetson snapped. "I offered him financial help on more than one occasion and I was told to get the hell out of his bar. He didn't want any help from King's family. If you think he didn't poison Jasper's mind against us, then you can think again, Wolfe. I wouldn't be surprised if he wasn't the mastermind behind everything that Jasper did. And I won't have you working for him." Stetson took the stance he always took when he meant business—eyes narrowed, fists clenched. "I damn well won't."

Wolfe should concede. Working for Uncle Jack was not fun by any definition of the word. All Jack did was yell at him . . . or blame his bartending skills for their lack of customers. Even though Wolfe didn't believe their uncle was the mastermind behind Jasper's crimes, he did believe Jack's hatred of King's family had spurred Jasper on.

And yet, Wolfe couldn't seem to quit the old guy.

Even if it meant being kicked out of the home he loved.

"All right, Stet," he said. "I'll be gone by morning."

## Chapter Nine

Gretchen woke up feeling like all was right in the world.

She had done it. She had won over Wolfe Kingman. All the Kingmans now considered her a member of the household. She didn't have to worry about being fired. Wolfe had even called the ranch her home.

Home.

Stretching her arms over her head, she released a long sigh of contentment and smiled up at the ceiling. She did a little happy bed dance before she threw back the covers and got up to get ready for church.

After she showered, she stood in front of her closet and frowned. She had wanted to dress the part of a housekeeper—or what she thought a housekeeper would dress like—so all her dresses were conservative and dull colors. There was nothing that reflected her happy mood. She finally settled on a light gray jumper that she wore over a white t-shirt. She thought about leaving her hair down. But after looking in the mirror, she decided church wasn't the place to release her wild mane. Once she finished braiding her hair, she grabbed her bible and purse and headed for the door.

As she neared the kitchen, she expected to hear the usual breakfast commotion. Gage and Adeline had left for Sagebrush Ranch yesterday after Adeline had gotten back from the Cursed Ladies' Auxiliary meeting, but Gretchen expected to hear the other Kingmans. Buck and Delaney's bickering. Stetson's stern reprimands. Lily's soft mediating voice. Potts' grumbling. And Wolfe's deep growl asking for seconds. But she didn't hear a thing. Not one thing.

She stepped into the kitchen and understood why.

No one was there. It looked like they had started breakfast. There were half-empty plates of eggs and bacon on the table and half-filled orange juice glasses and coffee mugs. But something must've interrupted it.

Probably a loose cow or a runaway horse.

She made herself a breakfast sandwich from the platters of bacon and scrambled eggs on the kitchen island before she headed out the door. The entire ride into town, she munched on her sandwich and sang along with the country songs on the radio. When she got to Holy Gospel, her great day continued. She found a parking space right up front, and then ran into Mystic Malone on her way into church.

"Good mornin', Mystic," she said. "Isn't it a gorgeous day?"

Mystic glanced up at the overcast skies and

laughed. "I guess it's all in your perspective."

"As my mama always says, 'If we didn't have cloudy days, we'd never appreciate the sunny ones.'" Gretchen glanced around. "Where's your grandmother? I hope she's not under the weather."

"She's fine. She just had one of her sleepless nights and slept in." Mystic hesitated. "Is everything okay out at the ranch?"

"Just fine and dandy. Why do you ask?"

"Hessy is convinced Wolfe working at Nasty Jack's has caused a rift between the Kingmans."

Gretchen stared at her. "Nasty Jack's? Wolfe is working at the bar? How long has he been working there?"

"Since last Monday. I thought everyone at the ranch knew. It's been the talk of my salon for the last week."

So Wolfe hadn't been out carousing. He'd been working at the bar. Gretchen didn't know why that made her so happy. But she couldn't help smiling as Mystic continued.

"No one, including me, thought a Kingman would go near the bar after what happened with Jasper. But Wolfe has always done the unexpected. Him getting a job there is certainly unexpected. Although if I was going to pick a career for Wolfe, bartending seems fitting."

Gretchen remembered the pride on Wolfe's face when he showed her the stables and the joy when he'd discovered Mutt was a good cutting horse. "I don't know about that. Ranching is in Wolfe's blood. I can't see him doing anything else."

Mystic's smile faded. "Sometimes what's in your blood doesn't always make you happy."

Before Gretchen could ask her what she meant, a woman yelled out.

"That's her! That's Wolfe's redhead."

Gretchen turned to the group of people walking into the church. At first, Gretchen didn't recognize the pretty blond pointing. But then, it hit her where she'd seen the woman before. Sue Ann just looked different with clothes on.

With a feeling that could only be described as jealousy, Gretchen glanced behind her to see what beautiful redhead Wolfe was interested in. But there was no one standing behind her. When she looked back at Sue Ann, she realized she was pointing at her. All the people walking into church were staring at Gretchen too.

She shook her head. "No . . . I'm not Wolfe's redhead. I'm just his housekeeper."

"You sure didn't look like you were cleaning house when I saw you naked in Wolfe's bathtub," Sue Ann said snidely.

There was a collective gasp, and Gretchen tried to explain.

"Oh, I wasn't waiting for Wolfe. I was just using his tub because my bathtub faucet sprung a leak."

Sue Ann snorted. "And Wolfe's was the only available tub in that big ol' castle? Tell that lie to someone else, sweetie. I've been there. I know the Kingmans have more bathrooms than the Kardashians."

"But Wolfe has the biggest—" Before she could

say tub, Sue Ann cut her off.

"Which is why you seduced him."

Mystic spoke. "That's more than enough, Sue Ann. I don't think casting stones is what folks should be doing at church on a Sunday morning." She glanced around. "Do y'all?"

Everyone looked guilty before they continued into the open doors. Gretchen just stood there stunned. She was Wolfe's redhead? The one everyone in town was gossiping about? A giddy feeling settled in her stomach before it spread across her face.

"I don't think there's any reason to be smiling just yet," Mystic said. "I might've stopped people from casting stones for now, but sooner or later, they'll pick them right back up and start throwing. Believe me, I know. It might be best if you skipped church this morning."

"But I haven't done anything wrong. If I leave, they'll think I have."

"Take my word for it. It doesn't matter if you haven't done anything wrong, this town can still find you guilty. I've spent my entire life trying to convince this town that I'm not like my grandmother. But people still stop me on the street and ask me to read their palms. The other day, Kimberly Reed wanted me to put my hands on her stomach and tell her what sex her baby is."

"So everyone is just going to believe I seduced Wolfe?"

Mystic studied her. She might not read palms, but she had the same piercing purple eyes as her grandmother. "Did something happen between you and Wolfe? I hate to ask, but I just have this feeling . . ." She shook her head. "I'm sorry. If you said nothing happen, nothing happened. The gossip will die down eventually. Probably when Wolfe starts seeing another woman. Which knowing him will be soon. Until then, keep your chin up and avoid Kitty Carson at all costs."

It was hard for Gretchen to keep her chin up. What started out as a great day was fast turning into a horrible one. She not only had to worry about the gossip spreading through the town, she also had to worry about it getting back to the Kingmans. She didn't want them to think she was a floozy who tried to seduce their brother. Or had already seduced him and was having sex with him. That would get her fired for sure.

Taking Mystic's advice, she didn't go into church. Instead, she headed back to the ranch. She thought about calling Adeline and telling her what had happened, but she didn't want to ruin her trip. Maybe Gretchen should tell Wolfe. He would set things straight with his family.

When she passed Nasty Jack's and saw Wolfe's truck parked in front, she quickly made a U-turn. The bar looked to be closed. There wasn't another vehicle in the parking lot when she pulled in. She parked next to Wolfe's truck and got out.

Nasty Jack's had to be the most pathetic bar Gretchen had ever seen. There was no big sign with a cute logo to greet customers. Just a scarred door with a scratched, dented doorknob that stuck when she tried to turn it. The inside of the bar was as unimpressive as the outside. The linoleum floor was worn. The tables and chairs scattered around were mismatched. And the brown vinyl seats of the barstools were torn. The only nice thing about the bar was the bar itself. It was long and solid wood, its high polished surface reflecting the multi-colored string of Christmas lights that hung above it.

"Hello?" She moved around the bar. "Wolfe?"

The click of boots had her turning to a stairway at the back of the bar. A second later, Wolfe appeared. His eyes widened when he saw her.

"Gretchen? What are you doing here?"

"I saw your truck in the parking lot and Mystic mentioned that you were working here." It was none of her business where Wolfe worked, and still, she couldn't help asking. "Why?"

He laughed. "That does seem to be the million-dollar question. It's too bad I don't have a million-dollar answer. It just seemed like the thing to do at the time."

"This is why Stetson was so mad yesterday."

He nodded. "And he's right. I should've told him. I was just being a chicken shit—pardon my language—by postponing the argument."

"Did you get things worked out?"

He looked confused. "So I guess you didn't hear."

"Hear what?"

"I moved out."

She stared at him in stunned shock. It was the last thing she expected to hear. "But you can't move out. Kingman Ranch is your home."

He smiled, but it wasn't anything like his usual

smiles. There was a sad slant to his lips. "Not anymore."

"I'm sure you can make up with Stetson," she said. "All you need to do is say you're sorry."

"I wish it was that easy." He waved a hand. "Come on up and I'll show you my new digs."

He led her up the stairs to a small room with only one window, and that window was painted over with black paint. Which explained why the room was so dark and depressing.

The double bed had a frame, but no headboard. The mattress was sunken in the middle like a deflated cake. The chenille bedspread was ragged and worn. The bed was the complete opposite of the massive solid wood, king-sized bed with the fluffy down comforter and Egyptian sheets in Wolfe's room at the ranch. The only other pieces of furniture were a wobbly-looking TV tray that held a lamp and a scarred chest of drawers.

Gretchen pinned on a smile. "Well, isn't this nice."

Wolfe laughed. "You are a horrible liar, Red. It's a dump." He glanced around, and his expression grew even sadder. "No wonder Jasper lost it."

"This was Jasper's room?"

He nodded and sat down on the bed.

Gretchen hadn't given much thought to Jasper Kingman. She'd only seen him a few times around the ranch and had never met him. When everything came to light, she'd thought of him as a bad man who had tried to hurt good people. She hadn't been upset over his death. She'd just been glad that Adeline and Stetson hadn't died in the fire with him. She hadn't thought about how his actions and death would affect the Kingmans. But it had to be emotionally devastating to discover a family member you loved and trusted had betrayed you so completely. It was easy to read the hurt and pain on Wolfe's face.

Gretchen searched through her mind for some of her mama's words of wisdom. But there was nothing that covered this. And maybe Wolfe didn't need empty words. Maybe he just needed to feel the support of a friend.

She sat down on the bed next to him, ignoring the lumps in the mattress . . . and the waves of heat that seemed to come from Wolfe's body. They sat there for a long time not saying anything. Finally, she couldn't take the silence for a second more.

"It's really not that bad. If you scraped the black paint off the window and got a new mattress and some bedding . . . maybe a few pictures . . . and a vase of flowers—"

Wolfe cut in. "Or just demolished it with a wrecking ball."

"Or you could come home."

He glanced over at her with gray eyes that, at one time, she thought held no emotions, but, now, she realized held too many.

"I'm not coming back, Red. I need to stay here for awhile."

"Because of Jasper?"

"And my uncle. He doesn't have anyone else to help him." He turned away and ran a hand through his hair. "He's probably going to lose the bar even with my help. I thought me working here would make the townsfolk see that the Kingmans weren't holding a grudge against Jack for what his grandson did. But it doesn't seem to be helping. They blame Jack for what Jasper did as much as Stetson does."

"But you don't."

He shook his head. "I guess I just don't think people should judge you by who your family is."

"Like they judge you?"

He rested his arms on his knees and cupped his head in his hands. "I'm not Stetson. I never will be. My brother is the responsible, hardworking king of Kingman Ranch. I'm just the irresponsible middle son who won't amount to anything."

"You're not irresponsible at all. You helping your uncle is proof of that."

He tipped his head and looked at her. "Are you sure I don't just want to work here for the booze and the women?"

"I know you're not a big drinker. As for the women . . ." She hesitated. "According to the townsfolk, there only seems to be one. The redhead. Which, thanks to Sue Ann, everyone at church just learned was me." The guilty look in his eyes said it all. "So you knew?"

He looked away. "Yeah. I was hoping you wouldn't run into Sue Ann before she left town. I'm guessing that didn't go very well."

"I might've been stoned to death if not for Mystic's intervention."

He sighed. "I'm sorry. It's my fault. I shouldn't have acted like you were waiting for me in the bathtub. I just wanted to get rid of Sue Ann so she wouldn't find out about my . . . little problem."

Just the mention of his "little problem" brought back the laundry room kiss and the feel of his hardness against her. Words just popped out of her mouth. "You don't seem to have that problem any more."

His gaze shot over to her and his eyes lowered to her mouth. A tingling heat settled in her panties and her breath left her lungs in a soft rush of air. When those smoky eyes lifted, they held a look that made Gretchen even more breathless. For one brief second, he started to lean toward her and she was sure he was going to kiss her.

But then he blinked and jumped up from the bed. "I'll fix it. I'll make sure everyone knows that nothing happened between us."

She nodded and stood on wobbly legs. "Thank you. Now I better get back to the ranch." She hesitated. "Are you sure you don't want to come with me? I made a cherry pie. My cherry is twice as good as my peach and apple."

Once again, his gaze lowered to her mouth. "I bet it is. But no sweet cherry pie for me, Red."

For some reason, she didn't think he was just talking about pie.

# Chapter Ten

"WHAT IN THE world is going on there? I'm gone for only a day and all hell breaks loose!" Adeline's voice was so loud Wolfe had to hold the cellphone away from his ear. That was unusual for his big sister. Delaney could break your eardrum, but Adeline only yelled when she was extremely upset.

He sat up on the edge of the bed and turned on the lamp. One glance at the dismal room had him turning it back off. "I'm guessing Stetson called you and told you that I moved out."

"No, Delaney called me. Stetson didn't want to get his butt chewed for kicking you out of the house."

"He didn't kick me out of the house, Addie. I chose to leave." After being given an ultimatum. But Wolfe wasn't about to mention that. He'd never made his issues with Stetson his siblings' problem. But Adeline had always been good at reading between the lines.

"You two got in a fight about you working at Nasty Jack's, didn't you? What were you thinking taking a job from Uncle Jack and not telling

Stetson? You know how upset he is over what happened with Jasper. All of us are."

"Are you?"

"What does that mean?"

He shouldn't have said anything. He didn't want to get in a fight with Adeline too. But now that he had brought it up, he couldn't take it back. "It just doesn't feel like anyone cares one way or another about what happened to Jasper."

"That's not true, Wolfe. We were all shaken up over Jasper. But I understand why you were shaken up the most. You were closer to Jasper than the rest of us. And I think it's commendable that you're helping Uncle Jack. I just wish you had told us what you were planning. Then maybe you and Stetson wouldn't have gotten into it."

"I didn't plan it. It just happened. Even if I'd told Stet, we still would've gotten into it. He thinks he can control my life. It's time I let him know that he can't."

Adeline sighed. "I don't like it, but I understand it. I had to set some boundaries with our big brother too. But moving out is pretty extreme, Wolfe. Kingman Ranch is your home."

Adeline sounded like Gretchen. They were both right. Kingman Ranch was his home. He hadn't realized how much until he'd left it. Last night had been one of the loneliest nights of his life. He had to wonder if loneliness was what had helped to drive Jasper insane.

He pushed the thought aside and tried to comfort his sister. "It's okay, Addie. I don't plan on leaving the ranch forever. I just need some time."

Adeline sighed. "Okay. Just don't take too long or I'll come find you and drag you home."

Wolfe laughed. "Deal." He hesitated. "There's something else I need to talk to you about, sis. I want you to promise me you won't blow a gasket until you hear the entire story."

"Okay, now I'm scared."

"It's not bad. There's just a little gossip going around town I think you need to know about." He told his sister all about Gretchen using his bathtub and Sue Ann spreading rumors around town.

"So Gretchen is your redhead?"

"According to Sue Ann, but it was just a misunderstanding. Not that the town will believe that."

Adeline groaned. "That's just great. This is going to ruin all my plans to get Gretchen and Pastor Chance together. There's no way the pastor will want to date Gretchen if he thinks she's in a heated affair with the town bad boy."

Wolfe didn't know why, but he suddenly didn't feel as depressed. "Maybe that's not a bad thing. I don't think Gretchen and the preacher are that good of a match."

"Why not?"

"I don't know. I just don't think they are. The preacher seems too stuffy and proper. Gretchen is a country gal who's funny and enjoys life too much to be stuck in a marriage with an uptight pastor. Did you know she's damn good with horses? She kept up with me on our ride without any problems. It would be a shame if she didn't have access to horses. Or a nice kitchen. She loves to cook. She makes the best pies I've ever had in my life. I can't see the preacher appreciating all her talents." The long stretch of silence had Wolfe wondering if they'd lost their connection. "Addie?"

"I'm here. I just didn't realize you and Gretchen had started getting along so well."

He grinned. "Yeah, it is kind of surprising. But Red has a way of getting under your skin."

Again there was a long pause. "She does, doesn't she? So what are you going to do about the gossip?"

"I'm sure it will die down once I start seeing someone else. For now, it might be best if you tell Gretchen to stay on the ranch and avoid town." A loud thump sounded in the hallway, followed by Uncle Jack's cursing. Wolfe jumped out of bed. "I gotta go, sis. I'll call you later."

After he hung up, he hurried into the hallway to find his uncle lying on the floor in his underwear.

"What happened?" Wolfe knelt down next to him.

"Oh, I just decided to take a little nap on the floor." Uncle Jack glared at him. "What the hell do you think happened? I fell. Now get me up."

Wolfe's gaze swept over his uncle's body. He hadn't realized Uncle Jack was so frail. "I don't think you should move until we see if you broke something."

"The only thing I'm going to break is your head if you don't help me off this damn hard floor."

"Fine. Have it your way." Wolfe carefully lifted his uncle into a sitting position. When he didn't notice any grimacing, he helped him to his feet. He intended to keep an arm around him until he was sure Jack was stable, but his uncle shoved him away.

"I got it, boy."

Wolfe had taken a lot from his uncle in the last week, and his temper finally snapped. "Like hell you have it! If I hadn't been here, you would've been lying on that floor until I showed up tonight."

"So what do you want? A gold star?"

"A simple thank you would be nice. Is it too much to ask for a little appreciation? Too much to ask to be treated like an equal rather than an idiot who doesn't have a brain in his head? I have ideas that might help you keep this place, but you're just like Stetson. You're too damn stubborn to listen!"

Uncle Jack's face turned bright red, and Wolfe figured he was about to explode. He did. Just not the way Wolfe thought he would.

"Then maybe you need to get louder, boy. You're going to run into a lot of stubborn cusses in your life. You can give up and let them have their way. Or you can keep fighting until you get yours!"

"Fine! You need to quit telling me how to do my job and shut the hell up. Nobody wants to come into a bar to relax and listen to you yelling and cussing at me. And we need to hire a barmaid. And a full-time cook. Good Eats is only open for breakfast and lunch. People want to eat out at night and have a nice dinner. Which is why Taco Tuesdays was your busiest night. And don't say we don't have any money to hire a cook and barmaid. I have money. And I would be happy to loan it to you until things pick up."

"I don't need your money."

"If you want to hang onto this place, you do."

Wolfe waited for Jack to continue arguing. Instead, his narrow shoulders deflated. "Why are you doing this, boy?"

"The same reason you protected Delaney the other night. We're family. I'm sorry about what happened between you and my granddaddy. But I'm not responsible for what King did. Just like you're not responsible for what Jasper did. So let's stop living in the past and move on."

Uncle Jack stared back at him for a long moment before he turned and headed to his room. "Don't hire a barmaid who smokes or a cook who can't make biscuits."

It wasn't the acceptance Wolfe had hoped for, but it was something.

Unfortunately, finding a barmaid and cook willing to work for his uncle would be as hard as finding a bartender. Wolfe figured he'd start with the cook who had already worked for his uncle and knew his sour disposition. When he finished showering and dressing, he headed to the only restaurant in town.

On the outside, Good Eats looked a lot like Nasty Jack's. The stucco was cracking, the paint peeling, and the only sign was the fading words that had been painted on the side of the wall a good fifty years earlier. But the inside was a homey diner filled with the scent of homemade bread and fried potatoes. Booths lined the front windows and gingham-covered tables filled the center space.

Since he was there to see Otis Davenport, Wolfe headed to the counter by the kitchen. As soon as he sat down, Otis's wife, Thelma, was there to hand him a menu and fill his coffee cup.

"Good mornin', Wolfe. What can I get you?"

"I came for Otis's pancakes and your sparkling conversation, Thel."

Thelma swatted him with the dishtowel she always had draped over her shoulder. "Don't waste your flirtin' on me, Wolfe Kingman."

"Flirting with a beautiful woman is never a waste."

Thelma laughed and called back to the kitchen. "You hear that, Otis? Wolfe thinks I'm a beautiful woman."

Otis peeked out of the service window and smiled his wide, friendly smile. "Hey, Wolfe! You trying to steal my woman?" Before Wolfe could answer, Otis waved his spatula. "Go ahead and take her. But be warned, beautiful women can make your life a livin' hell."

Thelma fisted a hand on her wide hips. "I'll show you a livin' hell, Otis Davenport."

Otis looked at Wolfe and lifted his eyebrows. "See what I mean." They all three laughed before Otis spoke. "What can I get you this morning, Wolfe? The usual—double stack of pancakes, three over medium eggs, and four sausage links well done?"

"That sounds about right. But I didn't just come in for breakfast." He smiled his thanks at Thelma for setting a tiny pitcher of cream next to his cup. "I came to see if maybe you'd think about coming back to Nasty Jack's. You can't judge Jack by what Jasper did, Otis."

"That's not why I quit working on Taco Tuesdays. I quit because that man is one mean son of a gun. When Jasper was there to run interference it wasn't so bad. But once Jasper passed, working for Jack was like working for a rattlesnake. I know the man was grieving, but I could only take so much of his orneriness. I can't believe you're working for him. Especially with as much as he hates your family."

"I think he acts like he hates people more than he actually does."

Otis shook his head. "Nope. I think he hates people. And life's too short to work for a man like that."

Wolfe sighed. "Do you know of anyone who might be willing to cook for us?"

"Us? You taking over the bar, Wolfe?"

It was a good question. What was he doing? He'd planned to just help his uncle out by bartending. Now suddenly he was living over the bar and hiring cooks. He didn't want to be a bar manager, but damned if that wasn't what he'd become.

"If you know of anyone who would be willing to help Jack out, I'd appreciate it if you'd call me."

"Sure thing, Wolfe. But I'm telling you right now, no one who knows your uncle is going to work for him."

Wolfe knew he was right. Maybe it was for the best if the bar closed. An eighty-one-year-old man didn't need to be running a bar.

After eating breakfast, Wolfe headed back to Nasty Jack's. A truck with Kingman Ranch stenciled on the side of it honked at him. With the tinted windows, he couldn't tell which ranch hand was driving, but he lifted a hand and waved anyway. He had to stifle the urge to run after the truck and hop into the bed.

Damn, he missed the ranch. He missed Buck and Delaney's arguing. And Potts puttering around in the kitchen. Lily talking about her fairies. Adeline and Gretchen giggling over something in the sunroom. He even missed Stetson ordering him around. He was so busy missing his home that he didn't notice the mail truck coming down the street toward him until it was too late to hide.

Kitty Carson zipped the little truck into a U-turn and pulled up next to him.

"Hey, Wolfe!"

Wolfe smiled. "Hey, Miss Kitty. How's the mail delivery going this morning?"

"Busy as all get out. Folks have already started their holiday shipping. I swear it starts earlier every year. I can tell you that my back isn't happy about lifting all those packages." She hesitated, and Wolfe knew what was coming. "So . . . I heard about you and that housekeeper of yours. I just wanted you to know that no one in town blames you. I knew from the first time I set eyes on her that she was trouble. It's the red hair. You can't trust a woman with natural red hair." She pointed to her blunt cut helmet of hair. "Mine is straight from a bottle."

"Now, Miss Kitty, Gretchen isn't trouble. She's a good Christian woman. You should know that because you see her at church every Sunday."

"That doesn't mean she's a good Christian woman. Hester Malone goes to church and we all know how evil she is."

As if on cue, Hester Malone's voice rang out.

"Don't you have anything better to do than spread gossip, Kitty Carson?"

They both turned to see Hester standing on her front porch. The morning sun reflected off her silver hair like a shining beacon of heavenly light . . . of course, her solid black clothes and angry glare didn't go with her angelic halo of hair.

Wolfe lifted a hand and started to greet her, but Kitty cut him off.

"How do you know that I'm gossiping? You can't hear me from there."

"I don't need to hear you to know what you're saying."

"Of course, you don't, you Satan's daughter."

"And what does that make you? Satan himself?"

Wolfe held up his hands. "Now, ladies. Let's not start throwing insults around. You're both fine, upstanding women of our community who serve the town in different capacities."

Kitty stared at him. "How is hocus pocus fortunetelling serving our community?"

"It's better than spreading false rumors!" Hester yelled.

"Nothing I repeat is false. Sue Ann said Gretchen was waiting for Wolfe in a tub of bubbles. If that isn't a plan of seduction, I don't know what is."

"Gretchen didn't plan to seduce me." And yet, every time she was around, she did seduce him. Yesterday, when she'd sat next to him on the bed, all he could think about was pushing her to the mattress and covering her lips and body with his. He needed to find another woman to take care of his needs and quickly.

"Then what in the world was she doing in your bathtub nek-ked as the day she was born?"

He started to explain, but Hester cut him off. "So what if Gretchen is trying to seduce Wolfe? That's none of your business, Gossip Girl."

"I just want to make sure that one of our own doesn't get trapped by the wicked wiles of a woman."

Wolfe waited for Hester to laugh at the ludicrous idea that a bad boy like him could get trapped. But Hester didn't laugh. Instead, she turned her sharp gaze on him. Which made him feel extremely uncomfortable . . . especially when she started rubbing the purple stone that hung around her neck.

"Wolfe is already trapped. But not by a woman as much as his fear."

## Chapter Eleven

THE KINGMAN RANCH just wasn't the same without Wolfe. Buck and Delaney didn't fight. Stetson didn't yell. Lily wasn't writing. Everyone just moped around with sad looks on their faces. Even Potts went on a cooking strike. He set out boxes of cereal for breakfast and store-bought lasagna for dinner.

"You want home cookin'," Potts said as he glared at Stetson. "Then you need to fix this mess you made."

Delaney and Buck blamed Stetson too. But after talking with Wolfe, Gretchen knew Wolfe leaving had more to do with Jasper than it did with his brother. His cousin's death had deeply affected Wolfe and he needed time to come to terms with it. He also needed the support of his family. While Gretchen felt uncomfortable bringing up such a sensitive subject with Stetson, she didn't feel that way with Adeline.

When Adeline called later in the week, Gretchen told her friend all about stopping by Nasty Jack's.

"You should've seen him, Addie. It just about broke my heart. I don't think any of us realized how much Jasper's death has hurt him. I certainly didn't realize it. I thought Wolfe was just this easygoing, fun-loving man who didn't have a care in the world. You told me he was sensitive, but I didn't believe it until I saw it with my own eyes. Have you seen that horse he's rescued? Why no one would've seen potential in that animal but your brother. The gentle way he handles Mutt is just heartwarming. And then there's the way he stepped up to the plate to help out your uncle. From what I hear, that man is as mean as a grizzly with a toothache. But Wolfe has given up his comfortable bed and home just to take care of your uncle. Now if that isn't a saint, I don't know what is. Right now, Wolfe needs as much love, support, and hugs as his family can give him."

When Adeline didn't say anything, Gretchen realized she'd been rambling. "Sorry, I got a little carried away. I'm just worried about Wolfe."

"I can see that," Adeline said. "And I totally agree with you. Wolfe does need our love and support right now. Of course, I'm not sure he's going to take it from his family. He and Stetson have this macho competitive thing going on. Buck and Delaney are his younger siblings so Wolfe feels like he has to be their tough big brother. And Gage and I won't be back for another week." She paused. "So I guess it will be up to you to give Wolfe support . . . and plenty of hugs and love."

Gretchen almost dropped her cellphone. She caught it and held it back to her ear. "Me? Oh, I don't know if that's my place, Addie. I'm just the housekeeper."

"You're much more than the housekeeper, Gretchen. You've become like family to us. But you're right. I shouldn't expect you to feel the same way."

"But I do! I've come to love your family. I just don't know if Wolfe would want me giving him support. My track record with helping him hasn't been very good."

"Those were all just little accidents and Wolfe doesn't hold them against you. In fact, when I talked with him the other day, he spoke glowingly about you."

Gretchen couldn't have been more surprised. "He did?"

"He certainly did. I wouldn't lie to my best friend."

A warm, fuzzy feeling settled in Gretchen's tummy. Not just about Wolfe's glowing remarks, but also about Adeline calling her best friend.

"I'll do it!" she said. "I'll call Wolfe and let him know he can count on me for anything until you get home."

"I think he needs more than just a phone call. I think you should stop by and check on him. I'd feel much better if someone was checking on him daily."

"Daily? Well, I guess I could stop by the bar in the evenings once I'm finished here."

"I was thinking more of the days when he's off and has time to spend with you. Don't worry about the housework. I'm sure the part-time maids can handle things. You just concentrate on my brother."

Before Gretchen could express her concerns about leaving the ranch during the day, the doorbell chimed.

"I need to go, Addie. Someone's at the door. It's probably Chance. He seems to be the only one who comes to the front door."

"Shoot!" Adeline said.

"What's wrong?"

"Uhh . . . I just stubbed my toe. Listen, Gretchen, I've been thinking about you and the pastor. And I just don't know if you make a good couple. He's much too . . . holy."

Gretchen laughed. "Are you saying I'm too much of a devil for the preacher, Addie?" Before Adeline could answer, the doorbell rang again and Gretchen hurried to the door. "I'll call you later. Don't you worry about your brother. I'll take care of Wolfe."

"I'm counting on it," Adeline said.

Gretchen slipped her cellphone in her apron pocket and pulled open the big oak door. Her heart dropped clear to her feet. It wasn't Pastor Chance. It was an attractive blonde in high heels and a fur coat she'd gotten from Husband Number Four.

"Mama?"

Delilah held out her arms and shimmied her big boobs and full hips. "In the flesh."

Gretchen's first thought was to slam the door and lock it. But she couldn't slam the door on her mama. No matter how much she wanted to. Delilah stepped inside and gave her a big hug, enveloping her in the scent of Chanel No. 5.

Gretchen had never cared for the smell.

She drew away. "What are you doing here, Mama?"

Delilah gave her a stern look. "I could ask you the same question. I thought you were back in Arkansas working at Kohl's. Not hanging out with your step-siblings in their Texas castle." She glanced around. "Lord, I forgot how big this place is. I really should've pushed for more money in the settlement."

"You have plenty of money, Mama. You don't need any more from the Kingmans."

"Now, Gretchen, what did I teach you? You can never have too much money." Delilah glanced down. "And where did you get that dress and apron? From an Amish yard sale? You look like the hired help."

Gretchen wanted to come up with some lie—anything to get her mother to leave. But she had never been good at lying to her mama. At least, not face to face. "I *am* the hired help," she said.

Delilah's eyes widened, and she placed a hand on her chest. The sunlight coming through the open door reflected off her huge diamond engagement ring. It looked like her mama had caught Husband Number Seven.

"A maid? My only daughter is working as a maid?" She fanned her face and staggered back. "I think I'm going to pass out."

Gretchen would've been concerned if it was anyone other than her mama. Delilah was a drama queen. "There's nothing wrong with being a maid. Grandma used to work as a maid."

"I swore me and my kids would never do the same. Which is why I worked so hard at making a better life for us."

"Marrying wealthy men is not a job, mama."

"Attracting wealthy men is. You don't have a clue how hard it is to stay fit and beautiful." Her mama always had a way with a backhanded compliment.

"So how did you know I was here?" she asked.

"I'm still paying for your cellphone. When you stopped answering my calls, I tracked your phone." Delilah shook her head. "I should've known you would come here. You seemed much too interested when I was telling you stories about this place. You always did love a good fairytale. Now get packed. We're leaving."

"I'm not leaving—"

"There you are, Gretchen." Stetson came out of the kitchen. "I was wondering if you washed my—" He froze and stared at Delilah. "Delilah?" His eyes narrowed. "What are you doing here? If you think you're going to get more money, you can think again."

"Now is that any way to greet your stepmama?" Delilah hurried over and pulled a stiff Stetson into her arms. "You look more like your daddy every day." She drew back and patted his chest. "But much firmer. And I didn't come here for more money. I came to get Gretchen." She turned to Gretchen. "I'm gettin' married, honey! That's what I came to tell you. It just won't be a weddin' without my baby girl as my maid of honor. So pack your bags and let's get going. As nice as this place is, I don't want my daughter being anyone's servant."

"Daughter?" Stetson stared at Gretchen. "You're Delilah's daughter?"

A thousand explanations were right there waiting to be said. But as Gretchen looked into Stetson's confused—then angry—eyes, she knew that not one of them would help her keep her job. Or her best friend. She'd lied to the Kingmans. She'd lied to Adeline. If not to their faces, then by omission.

Tears filled her eyes. "I'm sorry, Mr. Kingman. I'm so sorry." Before he could say anything, she turned and ran to her room. She only threw a few things in a suitcase before she headed out the kitchen door. She prayed she wouldn't run into any of the Kingmans. Or her mama. But Delilah was waiting by Gretchen's car and seemed completely surprised by the tears streaming down her daughter's face.

"Why in the world are you upset, Gretchen Maribel? I'm gettin' married and you no longer have to wait hand and foot on the snobby Kingmans."

"They aren't snobby." Gretchen tossed her suitcase in the back seat and wiped the tears on her cheeks. "They welcomed me with open arms and treated me like family."

"Family? You already have a family."

Gretchen should've just let it go. But she had spent all her life letting things go with her mama. Maybe it was time to point a few things out. "No, Mama," she said. "We were never a family.

You were a woman searching for an impossible dream and I was just extra luggage you had to drag along."

Delilah's eyes widened. "Why, that's just not true."

"What part? The impossible dream or me being extra luggage?"

"Both! You have never been extra baggage and finding true love isn't an impossible dream."

She sighed. "You're right, Mama. You found love time and time again. You just couldn't love them enough to stay and make it work."

Delilah didn't argue. She couldn't. "Well, it's going to work this time. Now let's get back to Dallas and start planning my wedding."

Gretchen felt like she had spent her entire life helping her mama plan weddings. And she was over it. "I'm sorry, Mama. But I don't want to help you plan another wedding. And I don't want to be your maid of honor either. To be truthful, I don't even want to attend the wedding."

"What do you mean? It won't be a wedding without you.

"It won't be a wedding with me either." She hadn't meant to be so brutally honest. But she couldn't hold in the truth any longer. "Weddings were never supposed to be big parties you invited all your friends to. They aren't about the reception. They're about the ceremony. A ceremony where you pledge to love one person, and one person only, for the rest of your life. You seem to be confused about that, Mama. And you made me confused about it for years and years. I thought you couldn't find a man who loved you enough. But now I realize that it's you who can't love them enough."

There was a long silence before Delilah spoke. "I love you enough."

More tears streamed down Gretchen's face. "I know, Mama. I love you too. But I can't take part in another wedding that will be over before the drycleaners get your wedding gown back."

"They do take a long time to get those back, don't they?"

Leave it to her mama to take that from the conversation. Gretchen couldn't help smiling. Delilah would always be Delilah. She couldn't expect her to be anyone else.

"So you're really not coming back to Dallas with me?"

Gretchen shook her head. "I can't, Mama."

Delilah cupped Gretchen's chin in her hand and brushed the tears from her cheeks. "The hardest part of being a mama is when you figure out that your baby isn't a baby anymore."

But it turned out that Gretchen was still a baby. She cried all the way into Cursed. She planned to drive through the town as quickly as possible, but her low fuel light was on and she knew she wouldn't make it to the next town unless she got gas. Thankfully, the gas pumps were automated and she wouldn't have to go in or talk to anyone.

She had just finished filling up and was paying with her credit card when a beat up red truck pulled next to the pumps behind her. A big ol' boy with a beer belly got out. He did a double take when he saw Gretchen.

"You're that gal who works as a maid for the Kingmans, ain't ya?"

She tried to blink back her tears, but a few leaked out. "I used to be their housekeeper."

The man grinned and moved closer, his eyes gleaming under the brim of his John Deere cap. "What happened? Didn't your bubble bath seduction work? Or maybe it worked and Wolfe just got tired of you." His gaze swept over her. "I got a tub. It ain't big, but I'm sure we can squeeze in."

Another truck pulled in on the other side of the pumps just as the man leaned closer and winked. "What do you say, honey? You want to take a bubble bath with Bubba? I like my women chunky."

Gretchen was about to give him hell when a fist connected with Bubba's jaw and he fell like an oak at her feet. Before she could get over her shock, Wolfe stepped between the pumps.

He gave Bubba one disgusted look before he turned to her.

"Bad day, Red?"

# Chapter Twelve

WOLFE WASN'T SURE what had happened. One day, he was a carefree, fun-loving cowboy with no responsibilities whatsoever. The next thing he knew, he was managing a failing bar, watching out for his grumpy old uncle, and babysitting his sister's best friend.

When Adeline had called him and told him Gretchen was Delilah's daughter, Wolfe had been more than a little stunned. He hadn't even known Delilah had a daughter. Of course, Delilah had only been married to his father for a few weeks before his father had died of a heart attack. During that time, Wolfe had been a wild teenager who was rarely at home and wanted nothing to do with his new stepmom. His father fooling around with every woman in town had been one thing. His getting married again had been another.

After their father passed, it was Stetson and the family lawyer who had to deal with Delilah's gold digging. Which was why Stetson was still worried Gretchen had ulterior motives for coming to the ranch. Wolfe knew a deceitful woman when he saw one. Gretchen was the complete opposite of deceitful. She was sweet and kind . . . and certainly didn't deserve to be treated like Bubba Burnett had just treated her.

Wolfe wanted to do more than just hit the guy. He wanted to beat him to a pulp. Especially when he saw Gretchen's green eyes were glistening with tears and her voice wobbled when she spoke.

"I've had better days."

He pulled a bandana out of his back pocket and handed it to her just as Bubba came to.

"What happened?" Bubba sat up and looked at him. "Did you hit me, Wolfe? What the hell for?"

Wolfe had to stifle the urge to hit him again. "For being disrespectful to a lady. Now apologize."

Bubba stared at him for only a moment before he got to his feet and took off his hat. "Sorry, ma'am. I didn't mean anything by it." He hurried back to his truck and took off in a puff of exhaust.

When he was gone, Wolfe looked back at Gretchen. He was used to her always being optimistic. Always having a smile and one of her mama's positive sayings. Her tears broke his heart. "Do you want to talk about it?"

She swallowed hard. "I lied to your family."

He nodded. "I know. Stetson called Adeline and Adeline called me. The Kingman phone tree is faster than Cursed gossip."

A tear trickled down her cheek. "I bet Adeline hates me."

"She doesn't hate you. She just doesn't understand why you didn't tell us." He hesitated. "And why Delilah's daughter would want to be our housekeeper."

"It's hard to explain." She used his bandana to blot her eyes before she looked at him. "I'm sorry that I lied. If you talk to Adeline, would you tell her that for me? Would you tell her that she was the best friend I ever had—the only friend I ever had—and I am so sorry I screwed that all up."

More tears rolled down her cheeks, and damned if Wolfe could ignore them. He pulled her into his arms. He had held a lot of women, but none had fit as nicely as Gretchen. All her full spots seemed to fill all his empty ones.

"Hey, now." He rubbed her back. "I don't think you screwed anything up. Adeline wouldn't have called and told me to make sure you didn't leave town if she was mad at you. She said for me to get you a room at the Malone house until she gets back from the Sagebrush Ranch and straightens things out with Stetson."

"So Stetson does want me fired."

"My brother hates surprises and worries about people trying to take advantage of the family."

She drew back. "But I would never take advantage of your family. Or do anything to hurt them."

He tried to tease a smile from her. "Are you sure? Because there were a few times when I thought you were out to hurt me." She started to deny it, but he held up a hand. "I'm teasing you. I know you wouldn't intentionally hurt anyone. I'll be happy to go back to the ranch with you and explain that to Stetson."

Gretchen shook her head. "I can't go back to the ranch after what I've done. I broke your family's trust. I can never go back."

He wasn't sure why the thought of Gretchen never going back to the ranch made him feel so depressed. Especially when there had been a time when her leaving was all he wanted. "Where will you go?" he asked.

"I don't know. I guess wherever I can find a job." She hesitated. "Maybe this time I will look for a job cooking." She handed him back his bandana. "Thank you, Wolfe. And don't stay away from the ranch too much longer. It's where you belong." She started to get into her car, when a thought struck him.

"Do you know how to make tacos, Red?"

She stared at him with confusion. "Yes. Are you hungry?"

"As matter of fact, I am. But that's not why I asked. I have a job for you. I want you to cook for Nasty Jack's."

"Oh, I don't know . . . I think I should leave Cursed. Once the townsfolk hear about what I did, they really will think I'm a manipulating seductress."

She had a good point. The townsfolk loved to think they were right. Especially Kitty Carson. Gretchen working at the bar might make them shun it even more. Still, he'd promised Adeline that he would keep Gretchen here until she got back. And Gretchen was the type of person who liked to be needed.

"Please, Red. I need you. I'm having trouble finding a cook and I'm hoping serving food will help save my uncle's bar. It shouldn't be too difficult. We'll only offer one dish nightly. We need to have tacos on Tuesday, but the other nights you can choose the menu. You can even make pies if you want to." He gave her his puppy dog look. "Come on, Red, help me out."

She hesitated for only a moment before she gave in. "Okay, but only until you can find someone else."

He rubbed his hands together. "Great! Let's head over to the bar and I'll show you around."

He was hoping Uncle Jack would still be upstairs when they got there and he'd have time to prepare Gretchen for meeting him. He wasn't so lucky.

"Who the hell is that?" Uncle Jack snapped as soon as Wolfe and Gretchen stepped into the bar. "If you think you're going to bring your whores here, you can think again, boy."

Wolfe was about to yell at his uncle for being rude when Gretchen spoke. "Oh, I'm not a whore. I'm your new cook, Gretchen Flaherty." She hurried over to the table and leaned down to give Jack a big hug. "It's a pleasure to meet you, Uncle Jack." She drew back and gave him one of her bright smiles. "I mean Mr. Kingman. Uncle Jack just sorta popped out. I never had an uncle before. My mama was an only child and my daddy had three sisters. Not one of them married." She laughed. "More than likely because they have ugly hair and freckles like me."

Uncle Jack stared at her for a long moment before he grumbled. "There's nothing wrong with red hair and freckles. My wife was a redhead."

"She was?" Gretchen's eyes turned sad. Pulling out a chair, she sat down and took Uncle Jack's hand. "I'm so sorry for your loss. How long has she been gone?"

Wolfe thought Uncle Jack would tell Gretchen that he didn't need her sympathy and to leave him the hell alone. But instead he hesitated for only a moment before he answered her question.

"Mary died twenty-one years ago."

"Bless your heart." She patted his hand. "That sounds like a long time, but it's not long at all when you're grieving a loved one. I bet she was a kind, lovely lady."

Uncle Jack nodded. "She was. She had to be kind to put up with a mean old coot like me. And she made the best biscuits I've ever put in my mouth." His eyes squinted. "You make biscuits?"

"I sure do, but mine probably won't come close to being as good as your wife's. Still, I'd love to make you some."

"They better be good or you ain't working here. And make a double batch." Uncle Jack glared at Wolfe. "That boy eats like a starving stray dog."

Gretchen laughed. "Doesn't he? I've never seen anyone eat like your nephew. But like my mama always says, 'There's nothin' wrong with having a good appetite.'" She got up. "Now I'll just go check in the kitchen and see if I have everything I need."

"I'll show you the way," Wolfe said.

"No need. I'm going to bet it's right behind those swingin' doors. You stay and talk with your sweet uncle." She winked at Jack before she headed to the kitchen.

Her dress was as frumpy as usual. That didn't stop Wolfe from staring as her curvy hips swayed back and forth beneath the neatly tied bow of her apron.

Uncle Jack snorted. "You didn't just bring her here to cook, did you, boy?"

Wolfe turned to find his uncle studying him with squinty eyes. "She's just going to cook."

He meant it. He wasn't about to get sexually involved with Gretchen. His life was complicated enough without adding to it. But every time he stepped into the kitchen to check on her, she was doing something that had his mind conjuring up a sexual fantasy.

Her rolling out dough on the butcher block island had a fantasy popping into his head of lifting her onto that island, hiking up her dress, and stepping between her full thighs. Bending over to pull the tray of baked biscuits out of the oven had his mind conjure a fantasy of taking all kinds of liberties with her round, curvy bottom.

By the time she carried the hot biscuits to the table, he was mentally cussing himself for bringing such temptation into the bar. He knew what the problem was. He hadn't had sex in weeks, and it was starting to take a toll. He needed to find a woman . . . who wasn't his sister's best friend. Or his new cook.

"Damn, girl," Uncle Jack said when he tasted a biscuit. "These are almost as good as my Mary's." He slapped a hand on the table. "You're hired."

Gretchen beamed as she sat down to join them. Watching her even, white teeth sink into the pillowy softness of a buttery biscuit had Wolfe squirming in his chair.

"You got ants in your pants, boy?" Uncle Jack asked.

"No, sir. I guess I'm just excited to go over the new menu with Gretchen."

Uncle Jack stared at him for a moment as if he knew he was lying before he got to his feet. "I have no desire to be part of any menu plannin'." He grabbed two more biscuits off the plate. "I'll be in my room if you need me." He looked at Gretchen. "I'll see you tomorrow. Don't be late."

"Yes, sir, Mr. Kingman."

"You can call me Uncle Jack." The nice gesture was ruined when he glanced at her dress. "But no ugly dresses. We wear western clothes in this bar. That includes jeans and cowboy boots. Hats are optional." He turned and shuffled to the stairs.

Once he was gone, Gretchen smiled. "He's quite the character."

"I wouldn't use that nice of a word."

"He's not that bad. He reminds me of Stepdaddy Number Three. His bark is worse than his bite."

It suddenly dawned on Wolfe that his father had been one of her many stepfathers. "What number was my daddy?" he asked.

"Five. Although I don't consider him a stepfather since I never got to meet him. I had just started college when mama called to tell me she'd gotten married in Vegas. She wanted me to come out for spring break and see the fairytale castle she was living in." She gave him a sympathetic look. "Then your daddy passed away. But I couldn't forget Mama's description of your beautiful home. And not just the castle, but the princes and princesses who lived there."

Wolfe laughed. "I wouldn't call us princes and princesses."

She smiled. "You sounded like them to me." Her smiled faded. "Or maybe just the perfect family. The kind who sticks together through thick and thin. That's why I came to the Kingman Ranch. I wanted to catch a glimpse of your fairytale family as much as I wanted to see the castle. When Addie mistook me for a housekeeping applicant, I went along with it because . . . I guess deep down I wanted to belong to that family."

The tears that shimmered in her big green eyes were Wolfe's undoing. He reached over and took her hand. "You do belong to our family, Red. Technically, you're my stepsister."

She gave him a wobbly smile. "You're older stepsister. I guess that means I get to boss you around."

Once again, his mind went straight to sex and her bossing him around in the bedroom. He quickly released her hand.

"What say we get to planning that menu?"

He tried to keep his thoughts pure, but it was hard when Gretchen sat so close. Every time he took a breath, his lungs filled with her scent. She smelled like fresh-baked biscuits and sweet flowery shampoo. And something hot and sensual that kept his mind in the gutter and his cock semi-erect.

"What do you think about Mondays doing pulled pork sandwiches?" she asked. "You can't mess up pork butt as long as you cook it low and slow."

The words "butt" and "low and slow" almost had him groaning. It took a second, and a little adjusting under the table, before he could answer. "Pulled pork sandwiches are fine."

She wrote pork sandwiches on the notepad she'd taken from her purse. "Tuesdays are tacos. And Wednesdays we could do chili and corn bread. Thursdays . . . meatball subs." She wrote that down before she glanced up and nibbled on her bottom lip. A lip he really wanted to nibble on too. "Do you think we should do spicy chicken wings on Friday? Or fried chicken?" When he didn't say anything, she glanced over at him. "Fried or spicy?"

"Spicy," he said in a hoarse voice.

"Spicy chicken wings, it is." She wrote it down. "Then Saturday I'll do hamburger sliders. And Sunday the bar is closed. What do you think about me making some pies every night of the week? I could do apple, chocolate cream, key lime, peach, chess . . . and cherry of course. Everyone loves my cherry pie." She picked up a biscuit from the plate and took a big bite, leaving her lips glistening with butter. No matter how hard Wolfe tried, he couldn't look away.

"Wolfe?"

"Hmm?"

"Are you listening?"

He wasn't listening. He wasn't listening to her . . . or his logical brain. All he could think about were those buttery lips and how much he wanted to lick them clean. He didn't realize he was leaning closer until her pretty emerald eyes widened. A man could lose himself in the crystal green. Wolfe certainly felt lost.

"W-W-What are you doing?" she stammered.

He stopped an inch away from her lips. "You missed a little butter, Red, and I thought I'd get it."

Her breath sucked in as he brushed his tongue over the soft fullness of her bottom lip. Whoever thought butter on biscuits was heaven had never tasted it on Gretchen. It was the most decadent, delicious thing he'd ever tasted. And he wanted more. He sucked her lip into his mouth, gently testing the plumpness with his teeth.

A sound came from the back of her throat. A sexy little noise that turned his semi-erection to a full hard-on. The rush of blood to his groin had him feeling lightheaded and needy.

He growled low as he went in for a deeper taste. She tasted of butter and biscuits and something he couldn't define. He leaned in closer. But he must have put too much weight on the edge of his chair. It came up off its back legs and flipped him onto the floor.

"Oh!" Gretchen jumped up and knelt next to

him. "Are you all right?"

He sat there stunned. Not just from his fall, but also from the kiss. He'd never felt so disoriented and confused. What was the matter with him? He had never had trouble staying away from women before.

A giggle had him glancing at Gretchen. Her eyes twinkled with laughter. "I think that's the first time you've fallen when I wasn't responsible."

But she *was* responsible.

She was causing him to fall, and he couldn't seem to stop it.

# Chapter Thirteen

"THANK YOU SO much for letting me rent a room from you," Gretchen said when Mystic opened the door of her basement hair salon. "I hope I'm not putting you out."

"Don't be silly." Mystic held the door. "Come on in."

Maneuvering her suitcase in front of her, Gretchen stepped inside. "I know you're probably wondering why I need a room."

Mystic smiled. "There's no need to explain anything, Gretchen. I'm not Kitty Carson or my grandmother. Your business is your business."

"Thank you." Gretchen glanced around.

Cursed Cut and Curl was the cutest salon she had ever seen. The white walls were striped with a soft purple. The floor was a black and white checkerboard. Two purple swivel salon chairs sat in front of black-framed mirrors and styling stations. At the back, two purple shampoo chairs reclined on black shampoo bowls. The waiting room had a white leather couch with fuzzy black and purple throw pillows and a brass coffee table filled with magazines and a purple ceramic bowl of hair product samples.

"This is adorable," Gretchen said.

Mystic beamed. "Thank you. It's a dream come true for me. I've wanted to style hair since I was a little kid—which explained all my bald Barbies and baby dolls."

"At least you chose to work on your dolls. I cut my own hair and ended up with no bangs. Of course, nothing can make my hair any worse than it is."

"That's pure nonsense. You have gorgeous hair. Of course, I've never seen it down." Mystic lifted Gretchen's braid. "May I?"

"Sure, but be warned. It's explosive."

Mystic pulled out the elastic band, then ran her fingers through Gretchen's hair to loosen it. "It's not explosive. It just needs a little shaping. After we get you settled in your room, I'd be happy to give you a trim."

"Oh, I couldn't ask you to do that."

"You didn't ask. I offered."

"Well, if you're sure. I guess I could use some shaping. Too bad you can't reshape my body."

"I wish I had a body like yours, instead of a flat chest and no hips." Mystic picked up her suitcase. "Come on, I'll show you to your room."

The bedroom Mystic rented out was behind the salon. It was a large room with a king-sized bed and en suite bathroom. Unlike the salon, the décor was more homey. The furniture was antique, and the curtains and quilt were covered in soft lavender flowers.

"I'll let you unpack and get settled." Mystic set

the suitcase on the chest at the foot of the bed. "I'll be in the salon when you're ready for your cut."

It didn't take Gretchen long to unpack. She'd left half her clothes at the ranch. Maybe deep down she was hoping she'd be able to go back. But she couldn't see how that was possible. The Kingmans would never trust her again.

But Wolfe did.

She had never thought he would be the one to come to her rescue when she needed a friend. She had thought he was the irresponsible Kingman. The one that no one could count on. She'd viewed him like her mama, flitting from one love interest to the next. But he wasn't like her mama. He didn't pretend to love someone when he didn't. He didn't make any promises he couldn't keep.

Gretchen glanced in the mirror over the sink and touched her lips.

Wolfe had kissed her.

Again.

The kiss in the laundry room she blamed on herself. She had initiated that kiss. But the kiss at Nasty Jack's Wolfe had initiated. He was the one who had moved toward her. When he said she had butter on her mouth, she'd thought he was going to use a napkin or his finger to get it off. She didn't think he was going to use his tongue. And his lips. And his teeth. Even now, she felt all breathless and warm just thinking about it. If he hadn't fallen, she didn't doubt that she would've had sex with him right there on the table.

At one time, she would've pushed the thought of having sex with Wolfe completely out of her mind. Not only because she didn't want to jeopardize her job, but also because she didn't think for a second Wolfe would be interested in her.

But the kiss proved he was interested . . . and she no longer had a job at the ranch.

She studied her reflection in the mirror. Was she seriously standing there trying to convince herself to have sex with Wolfe? She shook her head and sighed. She was being foolish. The kiss had probably meant nothing to Wolfe.

But what if it had?

The thoughts kept swirling around in her brain as she finished unpacking and then headed back to the salon. She was halfway down the hallway when she heard Delaney's voice.

"I think it's crazy too. But you know Addie. When she sets her mind to something, there's no changing it. And she's set her mind about Gretchen and—"

Delaney cut off suddenly, but Gretchen had already heard enough to know Adeline was never going to forgive her for lying. It took a real effort to hide her sadness and put a smile on her face when Mystic peeked around the corner. "There you are, Gretchen. Come on in. Delaney just stopped by to say 'hey.'"

Gretchen stepped into the salon and found Delaney stretched out on the couch with her boots crossed. "Hey, Gretch! So you're my stepsister. I guess that makes me Cinderella."

"More like you're the mean stepsister and

Gretchen is Cinderella," Mystic said.

Delaney scowled. "You're just saying that because you're Buck's best friend and I'm sure he's tainted your view of me. I'm as sweet as pie to other people, isn't that right, Gretch?"

Even though her heart was breaking over losing the trust of her best friend, Gretchen was glad Delaney didn't seem to hate her. "I'm sorry for not telling you the truth about my mama."

"There's no need to apologize. I wouldn't have claimed your mama either."

"Del!" Mystic yelled.

"What? I'm just stating the truth."

Gretchen couldn't argue the point. "She's right. My mama isn't exactly a mama to be proud of."

"She's still your mama," Mystic gave Delaney a stern look. "And people shouldn't talk badly about a person's mama."

"Fine!" Delaney looked at Gretchen. "Sorry, Gretch. But on the bright side, unlike Stetson, I don't think you're anything like your gold-digging mama."

Gretchen cringed. "Stetson thinks I'm like my mama?"

"Stetson jumps to conclusions quickly. And it didn't help that he heard the gossip about you being in Wolfe's bathtub."

"But it was all just an accident. Wolfe and I aren't having sex." But she'd been thinking about it. She shouldn't have been. Sex with Wolfe would only make Stetson think she *was* like her mama—chasing after a Kingman, hoping to get money. She refused to go down that path.

"Yeah, I know you're not," Delaney said. "Wolfe told me that you're just friends. He also told me he hired you to cook for Nasty Jack's." She pointed to the bag on the floor by the couch. "He asked me to bring you some boots. I brought the pair Buck bought me for Christmas because he's too ignorant to know that I wouldn't be caught dead in turquoise cowboy boots."

"What's wrong with turquoise boots?" Mystic asked as she guided Gretchen to the stylist chair. "I have a pair."

Delaney shrugged. "That's why I figured Gretchen wouldn't mind wearing them. I prefer my boots to be the color of horse shit. That way you don't have to clean them as much."

Mystic stopped in the middle of pulling a plastic cape from a drawer and stared at Delaney. "Get your dirty boots off my white couch!"

Delaney dropped her feet to the floor and sat up. "That's why I don't come visiting more often, Mystic. Your salon is too prissy."

Mystic laughed as she snapped the purple cape around Gretchen's neck. "That's not the reason. You're afraid of my grandmother."

"Well, who wouldn't be? The woman is scary as hell." Delaney hesitated and her eyes narrowed. "Although maybe I could use her help. Does your granny locate missing people?"

"She still hasn't located my mother so that would be a no. Why?"

"I met this hot cowboy the other night at Nasty's. Uncle Jack scared him off just when things were getting interesting. I was hoping to find out who he was and pick up where we left off. I think he could be this Cinderella's prince charming—he even has my cowboy boot."

"Your boot?" Mystic stared at her. "How did he get your boot?"

"He took off with it when Uncle Jack threatened him with a gun." She frowned. "I wish he'd taken my virginity instead. Those were my favorite boots."

Gretchen knew how worried the Kingmans were about Delaney's hurry to get rid of her virginity, and she couldn't help speaking up. "But if you don't even know his name, maybe you shouldn't be in a hurry to have sex with him."

"I know he's good-looking as sin and his lips are hotter than a jalapeño. That's all I need to know." Delaney rose to her feet. "Now if you ladies will excuse me, I'm going to go talk to Scary Hessy. Maybe she'll have a vision of my hot cowboy."

After the door closed, Mystic looked at Gretchen in the mirror. "That girl is going to get herself into big trouble. I can just feel it." She placed her hands on Gretchen's shoulders and squeezed. "I can also feel how upset you are about leaving the Kingman Ranch. But it's going be okay. I know it. Now let's get your hair shampooed."

Gretchen didn't believe for a second everything was going to be okay. Even though she knew she couldn't go back to the ranch, she had hoped she and Adeline could still be friends. But Delaney's words had erased that hope. Adeline had made up her mind about Gretchen and she wasn't going to change it. Which meant Gretchen needed to be gone from Cursed before Adeline got home. The thought had tears welling in her eyes. Luckily, they went unnoticed as Mystic shampooed and conditioned her hair. When she was finished, she directed Gretchen back to the styling chair where she combed out her tresses and started to cut.

With the way the scissors and hair were flying, it didn't seem like just a little shaping. Gretchen prayed she wouldn't turn out as bald as Mystic's dolls. After the cut, Mystic rubbed in a hair product before using a defuser. When she was finished drying Gretchen's hair, she spritzed on another hair product before she stood back.

A smile spread across her lips. "I knew it would look great." She spun the chair around to the mirror.

Gretchen was speechless. Mystic had tamed her wild locks into soft curls that framed her face and fell around her shoulders. Nothing had changed about her face, but it looked like everything had changed. Her features looked softer and her green eyes bigger and her freckles less noticeable.

Gretchen looked at Mystic in the mirror. "You are magical."

Mystic laughed. "I'm just a good hair stylist. Now come on." She unsnapped the cape and removed it. "Hessy should have dinner ready just about now."

Gretchen got up. "But you've already done so much. I couldn't impose any more."

"You're not imposing. Breakfast and dinner are included in your rent." Mystic folded the cape over the chair. "We'll go out the door so I can show you how to use your key. It gets stuck sometimes."

They stepped out the door of the salon and Mystic showed her how to jiggle the key to get it into the lock, then she locked the door and they walked around to the front of the house. Mystic stopped before she reached the porch steps and glanced down the street.

"It looks like Sue Ann is saying her goodbyes. I hear she's leaving tomorrow. Good riddance, I say."

Gretchen followed her gaze and saw Sue Ann standing in the parking lot of Nasty Jack's talking with Wolfe. Then Sue Ann wrapped her arms around his neck, and they weren't just talking. They were kissing.

For Gretchen, it was the hard, cold slap of reality she needed.

Wolfe Kingman's kisses meant nothing.

# Chapter Fourteen

WOLFE'S PLAN OF using food to get the townsfolk to patronize Nasty Jack's didn't work. Besides Delaney, Buck, and Mystic, no one from town showed up at the bar. But serving food did draw a bigger crowd from surrounding areas. By Saturday, word of Gretchen's pies had spread like wildfire. And Wolfe knew why. Her flaky piecrusts and tempting fillings were hard to resist.

Tonight, cherry pie was on the menu. As he stepped into the kitchen, the scent of buttery crust and hot sweet cherries engulfed Wolfe and made him ravenous. Or maybe it wasn't the scent that made him ravenous as much as the woman bent over the stove taking pies out of the oven.

Damn his uncle for telling her to wear jeans that clung to her curves. And damn Delaney for giving her sexy turquoise cowboy boots that filled Wolfe's head with visions of them wrapped around his waist.

He squeezed his eyes closed, in an attempt to wipe the image from his mind and spoke. "We need three more slices of pie. Two a la mode. And two orders of sliders."

Gretchen started, but surprisingly hung onto the cookie sheet with the pies and deposited it safely on the stainless steel counter before she took off her oven mitts. "I'll get that right up," she said as she moved to the flat top to expertly flip the small hamburger patties lined up in rows on the griddle. She might be a clumsy housekeeper, but she wasn't a clumsy cook.

She was efficient . . . and hot.

The hairstyle Mystic had given her only added to her hotness. She no longer wore her hair in a long braid. When she was cooking, like now, she wore it piled on top of her head with loose tendrils falling around her heat-flushed cheeks. And when she wasn't cooking, she left it down in a cascade of soft curls that begged for a man's touch.

Wolfe liked it up, but he liked it down even more. He was standing there fantasizing about running his fingers through the strawberry blond tresses when she glanced over her shoulder and sent him a quizzical look.

"Is there something else? Do you need some help at the bar?" She sent him a teasing smile. "It will only cost you a few busted glasses."

That was the thing about Gretchen that really threw him. When she wasn't filling his head with fantasies that made him hard as the cast iron skillets hanging over the island, she was making him laugh.

He chuckled. "I'll pass. Although you haven't broken anything yet."

"Give me time." She tipped her head and a tendril of hair caught on her bottom lip. His fingers twitched with the need to brush it away and test the plumpness. "You're hiding out, aren't you? Is Uncle Jack in one of his moods?"

"Actually, he's been rather quiet tonight. I think he doesn't want to acknowledge that I was right about needing a full-time cook. You've cast a spell on him."

Gretchen's smile got even wider. She had a dimple. A tiny little indention in her left cheek that caught his attention every time she smiled. "He just loves my biscuits."

Just the mention of biscuits brought back the taste of her buttery lips. Desire punched him hard in the gut. He wanted to kiss her again. He wanted it in a bad way and had for the last week. Thankfully, before he could do something stupid—like walk over and succumb to all his fantasies—she turned around.

"I'll get those orders right up."

Wolfe stood there for a moment trying to get a grip on his libido before he turned and walked out through the swinging door.

What the hell was happening to him? Why had he become so infatuated with Gretchen? Yes, she was attractive and had a damn fine body. But he'd dated beautiful women with voluptuous bodies before. Not one of them had him walking around in a constant state of arousal. Uncle Jack wasn't the only one Gretchen had casted a spell on.

And maybe it wasn't her outside appearance that had him spellbound. Maybe it was what was inside. Gretchen was real. There was nothing false or fake about her. From her wide smiles that made you want to smile back to her country words of wisdom everyone should follow. She had this positive outlook on life and a heart the size of Texas. He knew she was completely humiliated about lying to his family and would've loved to leave Cursed and never look back. But when he'd asked for help, she had put her feelings aside and helped him.

She was that type of giving person. The type that was always there when you needed her. She'd completely won over Uncle Jack. He still yelled at Wolfe, but he never raised his voice to Gretchen. She had won over Wolfe too.

He hadn't lied when he'd told her he liked her.

He liked Gretchen. He liked her more than he had ever liked any woman. Which was all the more reason to keep their relationship platonic. He had never hurt a woman intentionally, but he'd still hurt them. He didn't want to hurt Gretchen.

"What has you looking so glum, big brother?"

Wolfe pulled from his thoughts and glanced over to see Buck sitting at the bar. He moved behind the bar and walked down to his brother.

"Hey, Buck. What can I get you?"

"The perfect woman."

Wolfe laughed. While he didn't want anything to do with marriage, Buck's dream was to get married and have seven kids. His search for the perfect woman had started as soon as he'd graduated from high school. But he'd yet to find his one true love. Not from lack of trying. He'd dated about as many women as Wolfe had.

"Sorry, bro. We only serve liquor, sliders, and cherry pie tonight." He filled a glass with beer and set it on the bar.

Buck took a deep drink and wiped the foam off his mouth. "Actually, I'm here to see Gretchen."

Wolfe stopped wiping off the counter and stared at him. "Did Stetson send you to try and talk her into coming back to work at the ranch?" As much as Gretchen leaving would make Wolfe's life easier, just the thought of not getting to see her every day made him feel ... sad. It was a relief when Buck shook his head.

"Nope. Addie doesn't want Stetson hiring her back."

"What? Why?"

Buck shrugged. "Beats me. I can't figure women out. The only one I understand is Mystic." He paused. "And there are times I don't even understand her. We used to do everything together. Now she's so busy with the salon that she doesn't even have time to meet a friend for a drink."

Wolfe didn't care about Mystic not wanting to get a drink with Buck. He cared about his sister not wanting Gretchen to return to the ranch. "What did Addie tell Stet?"

"I don't know exactly. All I know is that she made Stetson promise not to hire Gretchen back." Buck leaned closer. "Speaking of Gretchen, now that she's not working at the ranch and doesn't appear to be Addie's friend, I'm thinking about asking her out. She can cook like nobody's business and is built like a brick shit—"

Wolfe reached across the bar and grabbed his brother by the front of his shirt. "Shut the fuck up, Buck."

Buck blinked. "What the hell, Wolfe?"

Realizing everyone in the bar was staring, Wolfe released Buck's shirt and lowered his voice. "I don't want you talking about Gretchen like that."

"I didn't mean anything by it, and I learned the term *brick shithouse* from you."

"Yeah, and I shouldn't have used it. Women aren't just bodies to drool over. And you're not drooling over Gretchen. Or dating her. She's not for you." It was weird how he used the same terminology he'd used after he kissed Gretchen in the laundry room. *I'm not for you.* Now Buck wasn't for her either. When had he become Gretchen's guardian angel?

"Why not?" Buck's eyes squinted. "Wait a minute, do you like Gretchen?"

"No-o-o." The word came out sounding like a grade school kid who had been accused of having a crush on his teacher.

Buck saw right through him and laughed. "Sure you don't." He held up his hands. "Okay, brother, she's all yours."

"She's not mine." He paused for only a moment before he confessed the truth. Not only to Buck, but to himself. "But I wish she was."

Buck stared at him as if he'd grown horns. "Are you telling me the infamous Wolfman, charmer of all women, has finally met a woman he can't charm into his bed?" He tipped back his head and guffawed while Wolfe glared at him.

"Watch it, little brother. I can still kick your ass."

The threat didn't seem to faze Buck. He continued to laugh while Wolfe filled a drink order. Even after he took the drinks to a table and came back, Buck was still chuckling.

"Adeline kept saying it was going to happen. I just didn't believe you'd ever fail at getting a woman."

The way Buck stated it had Wolfe bristling. "I haven't failed. I just haven't tried. Gretchen is different. Not only is she Adeline's best friend, but she's also the type of woman who's looking for a forever kind of guy. And we both know I'm not that."

"She told you that?"

"No. She told me she doesn't want to get married. But I think she's lying."

Buck's eyebrows lifted beneath the brim of his pushed-up cowboy hat. "So now you're Hester Malone and can read people's minds? Look, if she told you she doesn't want to get married, maybe she really doesn't want to get married. And who cares if she's Adeline's friend? Adeline got together with Stetson's friend without worrying about what Stetson thought." He grinned. "True, Stet kicked Gage's ass for it, but Adeline is less volatile than our big brother—unless you hurt Gretchen by not being up front with her about your intentions."

"I would never want to hurt Gretchen."

Buck leaned back and held out his hands. "Then what's the problem? She's a big girl who seems to know her own mind. If she's really not interested, she'll continue to say no. If she is, she'll say yes." Buck leaned his elbows on the bar. "Now let's talk about how weird Mystic has been acting."

Wolfe listened with half an ear as his brother rambled on about his best friend. While he had never taken advice from his little brother, Wolfe had to admit Buck had some good points. Gretchen was a grown woman. Why did Wolfe think she would get hurt? Maybe she was as interested in having a simple sexual encounter as he was? If the way she'd kissed him was any indication, she desired him. And he certainly desired her. He desired her like he had never desired a woman before. So why couldn't they have an adult sexual relationship where no one got hurt? He would lay his cards out on the table and let her decide.

He waited until the bar had closed and Uncle Jack had gone to bed before he headed to the kitchen. Gretchen was standing at the sink doing dishes when he walked through the door. He grabbed a dishtowel and moved over to help her. She startled and placed a sudsy hand on her chest, leaving a wet mark on her t-shirt that he couldn't seem to look away from.

"You scared me," she said. "I guess you got the bar all closed up."

He lifted his gaze to her eyes. His sister-in-law, Lily, had green eyes, but not the vibrant shamrock of Gretchen. Every time he looked in her eyes he wanted to book a flight to Ireland and lay in a field of clover . . . with Gretchen . . . naked.

"We need to talk, Red," he said.

"Is something wrong? Did someone complain about the pie?"

"No. Your pies are why the place was so crowded tonight. Everyone I talked with said they were here because a relative or friend had raved about the Cursed bar that served the best pie in the state of Texas."

Her cheeks blushed prettily and she went back to washing dishes. "So what did you want to talk about?"

"Us."

She froze and looked back at him. "Us?"

He had thought he knew exactly what he was going to say, but now the words seemed all jumbled in his head. He cleared his throat. "You have probably figured out that I'm sexually attracted to you." Sexually attracted wasn't close to what he felt for her, but damned if he could find any other words. He pushed on. "And if the way you kiss me is any indication, I think you're sexually attracted to me too."

She swallowed hard, but didn't speak.

He smoothed back a strand of hair that had come loose from her topknot. The simple act of touching her warm, flushed skin had his breath catching in his chest and his heart thumping erratically. He tucked the strand behind the shell of her ear. Beneath his fingers, he could feel the throb of her pulse. It echoed his. But he didn't know if his was from lust or fear. He had never feared an answer so much in his life.

"Do you, Red?" he whispered. "Do you want me as badly as I want you?"

It seemed to take a lifetime for her to reply. "Yes. I want you."

His shoulders sagged with relief and his heart swelled with something he couldn't put a name to. He started to pull her into his arms and kiss her when she stepped away and held up a hand.

"No." She shook her head. "I do want you, Wolfe. I want you more than I've ever wanted any man. But I realized something the other day when I saw you kissing Sue Ann in the parking lot."

He cringed and tried to explain. "I didn't kiss her. She kissed me. I don't have a thing for Sue Ann. I have a thing for you, Red." He wanted the words back as soon as he saw the hurt in her eyes.

"A thing?" she said.

"That came out wrong. What I feel for you isn't just a thing. I like you. I like you a lot. And I think we could be good together as long as you don't think . . ." He let the sentence trail off and she finished it for him.

"It's forever."

He nodded. "I'm not Mr. Right, Gretchen. I'm not anyone's Mr. Right. You don't want to be stuck with me forever."

"I'm not looking for forever, Wolfe. But I'm not looking for a one-night stand either. I need more than that."

A tight knot fisted his heart. "How much more?"

She smiled sadly. "More than I think you can give."

He wanted to say he could give her whatever she needed, but the words wouldn't come. Maybe because he knew they would be a lie. Like his father, he had never been good at giving to women. He was only good at taking. He didn't want to make a promise that he couldn't keep. He refused to lie to Gretchen.

She took off her apron and set it on the counter. "Goodbye, Wolfe."

He didn't know why the words felt like a dagger straight to his heart. Maybe because they sounded so final. Watching her walk away was the hardest thing he'd ever done in his life. But he did it.

He'd laid all his cards on the table . . . and she'd raised the bet.

If he wanted her to win, there was nothing left for him to do but fold.

And lose.

# Chapter Fifteen

After she left the bar, Gretchen's emotions were in a tailspin. Wolfe wanted her. Badly. When he had looked at her in that hungry way of his, she'd wanted desperately to feed him. She'd wanted to spread herself out like a five-course meal and let him devour her. It had taken all her willpower to refuse him and walk out the door.

He hadn't stopped her.

Which was a good indication she was right. He couldn't give her what she wanted. Not that she knew exactly what she wanted from Wolfe. All she knew for sure was what she didn't want. She didn't want to be like all the other women Wolfe had gone to bed with—easily forgotten when the morning sun slipped over the horizon. She didn't just want sex with him.

Not that it was easy rejecting a night of lovemaking with a man who set her on fire with just one glance of his smoky gray eyes.

She spent most of the night tossing and turning . . . and regretting her decision. By morning, she was even more of a wreck. Hoping for a distraction from her riotous thoughts, she got up and got dressed and headed to church with Mystic and Hester.

Not surprisingly, she still seemed to be the center of town gossip. As she walked into the church, people looked at her and whispered behind their hands.

"Damn gossiping fools," Hester grumbled.

"Watch your language in church, Hessy," Mystic chastised.

"God damns people. What do you think hell is for? I'm just giving him some direction." Hester gave Gretchen's arm a squeeze as they sat down in a pew. "Don't you worry about these yahoos. They'll come around. I saw it in the cards last night. I also saw the Ace of Wands which means sexual fun is in your near future."

"Hessy!" Mystic hissed under her breath, but Hester only winked at Gretchen as the service started.

Once the opening hymn finished, Gretchen was surprised when Reverend Floyd introduced Chance as the new pastor who would be taking over for him when he retired in a few months. She hadn't realized Chance was back in town. As he stepped up to the pulpit, she had to admit he was a handsome man. He was also a charming speaker who wove humor and clever analogies into his sermon.

"I think we found a good man to lead our flock," Hester said as they were filing out of the church.

"I thought you saw devil horns coming out of

Chance's head," Mystic said.

"I did. But the man who gave the sermon today isn't the same man I met the other day."

Before Gretchen could ask her what she meant, Hester saw Kitty Carson and headed toward her.

Mystic sighed. "I better go make sure they don't kill each other."

After she left, Gretchen felt a light touch on her arm and turned to see Chance standing there with a friendly smile.

"How did I do?"

"It was a wonderful sermon, Chance."

"Thank you. I'm glad you came. I planned to call you this afternoon to see if you wanted to go to dinner tonight to discuss the Cowboy Ball."

The last thing Gretchen felt like doing was going to dinner. But maybe this was the distraction she needed to stop thinking about Wolfe.

"That would be lovely," she said.

"Great. I'll pick you up around six."

On the way home from church, she noticed Wolfe's truck was missing from Nasty Jack's parking lot. She couldn't help wondering if he'd gone to find a woman who didn't expect more than just one night of great sex. The thought of Wolfe in the arms of another woman had Gretchen's emotions in even more of a tailspin. After she changed out of her church clothes, she headed over to the bar and started baking pies.

Baking comforted her like few things could and the countertops in the kitchen were soon filled with a variety of pies.

Uncle Jack came into the kitchen and chatted

with her for a while. But after he'd eaten a big piece of blueberry pie, he headed upstairs to take a nap. So when the door of the kitchen swung open, Gretchen figured it could only be one person. She took a deep breath and pinned on a smile before turning.

But it wasn't Wolfe who stood in the doorway. It was Stetson.

He pulled off his cowboy hat. "Hi, Gretchen."

She turned off the stove to let the apple pie filling she'd made cool. "Mr. Kingman. What a surprise. Would you like some pie?" She waved a hand around at all the pies on the counters. "We have plenty."

His eyebrows lifted as he looked around. "I'll have a piece of that chess pie if it's not too much trouble."

"No trouble at all. Sit right down on that stool and I'll cut you a piece."

Taking a seat, he hooked his hat on his knee and watched while she cut into the pie. "Chess pie was my mother's favorite."

She plated the pie, then got a fork and set both down in front of him. "Potts mentioned that your mama loved pie. I hope this doesn't bring back bad memories."

"Actually, it brings back good ones." He cut into the pie and took a big bite. His eyes widened. "No wonder everyone is talking about Nasty's new pie baker."

"Not everyone. The townsfolk still won't come here. Pie or no pie." She sat down on a stool across from him. "I'm assuming you're here to talk to

Wolfe. Uncle Jack said he went into Amarillo to get some things. But I'm sure he'll be back soon." She hesitated. "He's missed you."

"I doubt that. He hasn't been back to the ranch once since he left."

She had always had a healthy respect for the head of the Kingman Ranch. And she still respected Stetson. But there were some things that needed to be said. "And you haven't been here until today. So maybe you've both been a little too stubborn."

She thought her bluntness would anger him. Instead, he laughed. "You sound like Lily. She's always calling me a stubborn fool."

"I hope you're here to change that."

He nodded. "I want my brother home. And you. I don't care what Adeline wants. It's time."

Gretchen's heart sank. "Addie must hate me for lying to her."

He shook his head. "Adeline doesn't hate you. She got some crazy notion in her head that you and Wolfe care about each other and will end up figuring that out if we give you enough time together."

Gretchen was relieved her friend wasn't mad at her, but she was shocked to hear about her plan. She knew Adeline had been in matchmaking mode ever since Gretchen had told her about Hester's prediction, but she had never dreamed Adeline wanted to pair her with Wolfe.

"Me and Wolfe?" she said.

"I don't know where she got the idea. Wolfe is not the marrying kind. He has always struggled with showing his emotions. Even with his family."

"I don't agree," Gretchen said. "I think Wolfe shows his emotions all the time. He just doesn't show them like other people do. He shows them by actions. He helped your uncle when no one else would. He brought home a horse that no one else wanted. And he was there for me when no one else was. I think he would make someone a wonderful husband. You need to give him credit for the good man he is."

Stetson studied her for a long moment before he spoke. "You're right. I don't give Wolfe enough credit." He glanced around. "He made this bar work without any help from the townsfolk."

"Or his big brother. If you had supported the bar, the townsfolk would've followed."

He glanced back at her. "Maybe I was afraid that if the bar succeeded, then Wolfe would never come home. Maybe I still am."

"Tell him that, Stetson. Tell him that you miss him, and you want him back at the ranch. When mama first showed me a picture of the Kingman castle, I thought for sure cold, snobby princes and princesses lived there. But then I came and discovered a warm, loving family. A family who squabbles and disagrees, but always finds a way back to each other. Make sure Wolfe finds his way back."

Stetson studied her. "Adeline was right. You are a good person, Gretchen Flaherty. I hope you'll come back to the ranch too."

Going back to the Kingman Ranch was what

she thought she wanted. But if that was true, then why wasn't she jumping at the chance? Stetson wanted her to come back. Adeline wasn't mad at her. There was only one thing keeping her from accepting. Wolfe. Things had changed between them. If she went back, she knew she would eventually succumb to temptation. She couldn't go back to the ranch. And she couldn't keep working at the bar either. It was time to leave Cursed and find another home.

She smiled. "Thank you, but I've discovered that I don't want to be a housekeeper. I want to be a baker."

Stetson nodded. "Well, you're damn good at it. Tell Wolfe I was here."

She packed up the rest of the chess pie and handed it to him. "Tell him yourself. We open tomorrow at four. And on your way out be sure to say goodbye to Uncle Jack. If he's not at his table, he'll be upstairs in his room."

Stetson took the pie and squinted at her. "No wonder you're best friends with my sister. You both know how to get what you want."

He was wrong. She didn't know how to get what she wanted. It was time to accept it and move on. After she finished baking the pies and cleaning up, she headed back to the Malone's to get ready for her date with Chance. She should've canceled. All through dinner, it was a struggle to smile and act like everything was okay when her heart felt like it had been peeled and cored like an apple. It hurt even more when she told Chance she wouldn't be able to help with the Cowboy

Ball because she was leaving town.

"I'm sorry to hear that," he said. "Do you want to talk about it? I'm a good listener."

Not wanting to burst into tears in front of the new preacher, she shook her head. "Sometimes you just need a change."

When they got back to the Malones', he walked her to the basement door. She worried he would try to kiss her. Instead, he gave her a tight hug.

"Good luck, Gretchen Flaherty. If you ever need a friend to talk to, just call."

After he walked away, she took her key out of her purse to unlock the salon door. But it wasn't locked. Mystic must have forgotten to lock up. Gretchen pushed it open and stepped inside the dark salon before locking it. A deep, growling voice had her dropping the keys and her purse.

"Did you have fun?"

Gretchen turned. With the moonlight coming in through the door, she could just make out Wolfe's large form sitting in one of the styling chairs.

"What are you doing here?" she asked.

He got up from the chair and moved toward her until he was standing only a breath away. The moonlight coming in through the glass door fell across one side of his face, gilding his dark hair as silver as his eyes. When he spoke, his warm, beer-scented breath rushed over her and his deep rumbling voice made her heart feel suspended in her chest.

"How much more, Red?" When she didn't answer, he lifted a hand and cradled her jaw in the warmth of his palm. "How much more do you want from me?" His eyes were intense and filled with what looked like pain. "You don't want to be another one of my women. Well, baby, you're not. No woman has ever tied me in knots like you do." His thumb brushed over her bottom lip, sending a shower of heat cascading through her. "You consume all my thoughts. All my wants. All my desires. You've gutted me. And you want more?"

His hand slid from her jaw into her hair and he grabbed a fistful, tipping her head back as his glittering gaze locked with hers. "Then have all of me."

His mouth descended as he drove her back against the door. Her body didn't even register the cold of the glass. All she could register was the heat of Wolfe's kiss. He wasn't gentle. He was ravenous. He hungrily pulled and nipped and sucked on her lips as if he couldn't get enough.

His hand slipped beneath her shirt and, with one deft flick, he unhooked her bra. He took her freed breast in hand, molding and shaping her to his palm. He pinched her nipple and a zing of tingling heat zipped straight to the spot between her legs. She moaned her need and he released her lips and stripped her dress over her head, then slipped her bra from her arms.

She waited for him to start kissing her again. Instead he turned her to the moonlight shining in through the door and stepped back. Embarrassed about having her body so fully exposed, she tried to cover herself. But he caught her arms.

"Don't. You're too beautiful to hide."

As she stood there bathed in moonlight while he looked his fill, she noticed the fast rise and fall of his chest beneath the cotton of his shirt and the hard ridge in the fly of his jeans. Suddenly, she felt beautiful.

Beautiful enough to entice a wolf.

He'd offered her everything. And she wanted to offer him the same.

She slipped off her flats and reached for the waistband of her panties. Before they had even slipped to the floor, Wolfe released a deep growl and pulled her back into his arms.

His kisses became slower—deeper—as his hands slid over her body, stroking, cupping, and enflaming. Wanting to give him the same enjoyment he was giving her, she tugged his shirt up over his head. In the moonlight, he looked like an alabaster statue of a Greek god. A tattooed Greek god.

She ran her fingertips over the wolf tattoo, tracing its thick fur, broad nose, and sharp fangs. "Did it hurt?"

"Yes." He gritted his teeth. "But not as bad as trying to hold back from taking you right here on the floor."

She lifted her gaze to his. "I make you hurt?"

"You've made me hurt from the first moment I saw you in that bubble bath."

She smiled. "Good."

He laughed. "And here I thought you were such a sweet little ol' country gal, Red."

She slid a finger down his stomach to the button of his jeans. She flicked it open and pulled down his zipper. His breath hitched as she slipped her hand inside his briefs. "Not so sweet."

His breath rushed out as she stroked him. On the third stroke, he encircled her hand with his and showed her what he liked as he kissed her until she was limp and mindless. Then he swept her up in his arms and carried her to the bedroom where he laid her on the bed and finished getting undressed.

He had the most perfect body she'd ever seen in her life. When he leaned over to pull off his jeans, she couldn't help reaching out to touch his fine butt. He stilled as she ran her hand over each muscled cheek. When he turned, it was obvious that he'd liked it. His hard length jutted out proud and strong. She went to reach for him, but he took her ankles and tugged her to the edge of the bed, kneeling between her spread thighs.

In the moonlight streaming in the window, his smile flashed. "A true redhead." He dipped his head and kissed her.

From that moment on, everything became a blur. His tongue tasted with soft sweeps as his mouth feasted with hungry pulls. Time ceased to exist. There was only Wolfe and the moans and trembles he drew from her body. She had become a wolf's feast and she prayed the feasting would never end. He took her out of her body and sent her spiraling into an orgasm so intense, all she could do was tighten her fingers in his thick hair and hold on.

Through her haze, she chanted one word. "Wolfe. Wolfe. Wolfe."

## Chapter Sixteen

Watching Gretchen reach climax was the most beautiful thing Wolfe had witnessed in his life. With her head tipped back and her eyes closed, she chanted his name in a low, sexy groan that touched something deep inside him.

It wasn't like women hadn't said his name before in bed. They'd screamed it, panted it, squealed it. But they'd never said it like it was a mantra. Like the word meant something more to her than just a name. Like he meant something more. When her orgasm ended and she stopped saying his name, he felt a void. So he gave her another orgasm. And another. Just so he could hear her say his name over and over again.

When he finally slipped deep inside of her warm, tight body, her name came out of his mouth like a prayer. "Gretchen." He repeated it with each thrust. Although he didn't last long. On the fourth thrust, he tumbled headfirst into the best orgasm of his life.

When the last of the muscle-twitching sensations had subsided, he fell back on the pillows, stunned. He had always prided himself on his stamina. But he had no stamina or willpower with Gretchen. He'd wanted to stay away from her. No matter how hard he tried, he couldn't. Now that he had tasted her, had been deep inside of her, he knew there was no way he could keep from doing this again and again. He needed her. He needed her like he had never needed another woman.

And it scared the shit out of him.

But it also made him happy. Happier than he'd felt in a long time. When she placed her head on his chest and snuggled against him, that happiness grew and bloomed into a warm feeling of pure joy. Words pushed at the back of his throat. Words he was too scared to release. So instead, he said something stupid.

"Thank you."

She pressed her lips against his chest. They felt like a brand, searing straight through the skin and muscle and bone to where his heart beat fast and steady. "I never knew it could be like that."

"Me either."

She lifted her head and sent him a flirty smile. "I bet you say that to all the girls."

The thought that Gretchen considered herself one of many bothered him. He had never given much thought to the number of women he'd been with or his reputation as a ladies' man. Sex was something that was offered to him and something that he took.

Until now.

Now, he realized he had cheapened something

that shouldn't be cheap. Because he had, there was no way he could ever make Gretchen believe how special this night had been to him. How special she was to him.

While he was lost in his thoughts, she kissed his chest again. "It's okay, Wolfe."

He lifted her chin until her green gaze met his. "No. It's not okay. This was different, Gretchen. I mean it. I can't change the fact I've been with a lot of women. But what just happened was a first for me."

A skeptical look entered her eyes. "And just what made it special?"

He brushed his thumb along her soft cheek. "You."

Her eyes softened in a way that made his breath catch. "I feel the same way. You're special, Wolfe."

There was no way to describe the way Gretchen's simple words made him feel. No one had ever told him he was special. He'd always just been the bad boy. The Kingman most likely to fail. He didn't know what to say. Or how to express his gratitude. So he kissed her. The kiss soon grew heated, and she moved on top of him and whispered against his lips.

"I want you."

He nipped at her lips. "I want you too. But you'll have to give me a second, baby. I need a little recovery time."

She drew back, a mischievous twinkle in her eyes. "And here I thought you no longer had a problem getting it up. You know there are little pills for—"

Before she could finish he had her flipped to her back and straddled her. "Why you little smartass." He tickled her ribs until she giggled uncontrollably and fidgeted beneath him.

"Stop, Wolfe!"

But seeing her eyes twinkle and her face crinkled up with laughter made him realize that he never wanted to stop making this woman laugh. He gave her a few more tickles before he slid his hands up her ribs and cradled her sweet breasts.

It turned out that he didn't need a lot of recovery time, after all.

But this time, there was no rush. He took things slow, learning all her voluptuous curves and hidden valleys. Her body became his playground and he played until they were both spent. Then he pulled her close and they slept.

Around dawn, he woke up to her snuggled against his side. He wanted to stay right there in her arms all day. But Mystic and Hester would worry if Gretchen didn't show up for breakfast and then they'd come to investigate. Mystic told Buck everything. And Wolfe wasn't ready for his family to know just yet. He wanted time with Gretchen free of any outside pressures or distractions. He wanted to keep her all to himself for a while.

Tenderly, he shifted her to the other side of the bed. She grumbled a little but then snuggled into the pillow and kept sleeping. He got dressed and placed a kiss on her forehead before he headed out the door. As he crossed the Malone's dew-drenched front lawn, he admired the sun peeking over the horizon. It was going to be a beautiful day.

"We'll get a little rain later."

The words had him freezing in mid-stride and turning to see Hester Malone sitting on the front porch

He glanced up at the clear sky. "Are you sure about that, Hessy?"

"Even the sunniest day can turn stormy. But no matter how dark it gets, you need to remember the sun is still shining behind those clouds."

He wasn't sure what she was trying to tell him. He never had understood Hester Malone. "Yes, ma'am."

She rose from her rocking chair and moved to the edge of the porch. "She's not your usual type of woman."

He was going to play dumb, but then thought better of it. Especially when he was sneaking across her lawn at dawn. "No, ma'am, she's not. And I'd sure appreciate it if you would keep this between the two of us. I don't want her reputation hurt any more than it already is."

Hester studied him. "Everyone thinks you're such a bad boy. I don't agree. You never were a bad boy. Just the middle son who didn't know quite where he fit into the scheme of things. Looks like you've found a spot. Every town needs a bar where folks can gather and talk about their troubles."

"If we can't get the townsfolk to stop holding a grudge, Nasty Jack's won't be here much longer."

She rubbed the stone hanging around her neck.

"Like I said, a storm is coming that will set the town straight."

Wolfe hoped her prediction was true. "Good seeing you, Hessy." He headed across the street to the bar.

When he stepped in the door, he heard his uncle yelling. "What do you mean I have to wait twenty-four hours to file a missing person's report? I don't care about a damned report. My nephew is missing. I want you to find him, you bumbling idiot!"

Wolfe moved around the corner and found his uncle sitting at the bar talking on the phone. The concern on his face was easy to read. So was the anger when he glanced up and saw Wolfe. He slammed the phone back in the cradle. "Where the hell have you been, boy?"

Wolfe hadn't thought his uncle cared one way or the other about him. Obviously, he'd been wrong. He couldn't help but smile. Which made Jack even madder.

"You think it's funny, boy? I thought something happened to you. I thought you might be lying dead somewhere like . . ."

Wolfe's smiled faded. "I'm sorry, Uncle Jack. I should've called or left a note to let you know I was going to be out all night. I didn't think you cared."

Uncle Jack scowled. "I don't care. I just wanted to know if I needed to hire another bartender."

Jack's inability to express his feelings reminded Wolfe of himself. Maybe it was time to let their emotions out. He walked over and hugged his uncle. "I care about you too, Uncle Jack."

Uncle Jack allowed the hug for only a second before he shoved him away. "Don't go gettin' all mushy on me, boy."

Wolfe grinned. "Never, old man. Now let's talk about getting a sign for out front."

Wolfe ended up arguing with his uncle over a sign for a good fifteen minutes before he gave up and went upstairs to take a shower. When he came back down, Jack was sitting at his usual table enjoying a stack of pancakes covered in maple syrup. Since his uncle didn't cook that could only mean one thing.

Gretchen had arrived.

With his stomach feeling like he'd swallowed a herd of butterflies, he walked into the kitchen and found her standing at the butcher block island, rolling out piecrust. Her hair was piled up on her head and there was a smudge of flour on the butt of her jeans. She was singing along with the radio. She had a pretty voice—husky and sexy. He stood there listening and looking his fill for a few minutes before he walked over and put his arms around her. He buried his nose in her neck and breathed deeply of the scent of pastry, soap, and woman.

"Good mornin'," she said in a breathless voice. He hoped he was responsible for taking her breath away. He brushed a kiss over her neck before he turned her around. Her cheeks were flushed and her green eyes twinkled. Just looking at her made emotion deepen his voice.

"Good mornin'." He kissed her. Her lips welcomed him with a lushness that made his knees weak. When he drew back, her eyes were soft and held something that made his heart thump like crazy. "You're here early."

"I thought I'd get some pies baked."

He glanced around at all the pies on the counter. "I don't think we need more pies, baby."

"Oh, but we do." She started talking excitedly. "Last night, after we made . . . had sex." His brow knotted and he wanted to correct her, but she hurried on. "I had this epiphany. If pies helped our neighbors to accept Mama, then they'll certainly help the townsfolk to quit holding a grudge against Uncle Jack."

"But none of the townsfolk will come into the bar to try your pie."

"Then we'll just have to take the pies to them. I'm going to make a pie for every prominent member of Cursed—including business owners and the Cursed Ladies Auxiliary Club."

"How will that make them forgive Uncle Jack?"

"Uncle Jack will be the one delivering them. I'll go with him, but he'll be the one handing over the pies."

Wolfe hated to burst her bubble, especially when she looked so excited, but he didn't want her getting her hopes up either. "Umm . . . sweetheart, I know you're only trying to help, but Uncle Jack delivering pies has disaster written all over it. That's if you can even talk him into doing it."

"He'll do it. He just needs a little persuading. He doesn't have to say much. The pies will speak for themselves."

Since it looked like she had her heart set on it, Wolfe gave in. "Okay. I'll help you persuade him. Although you probably won't need any help. You are damn good at persuasion." A smile tickled the corners of his mouth. "You certainly persuaded me to go to bed with you."

Her eyes widened. "Me? You were the one who showed up at the Malone's with your come-hither gray eyes and sexy scruff begging for my attention."

He released his smile. "I'm still begging for your attention. If I'd known that you thought my scruff was sexy, I wouldn't have shaved this morning."

She touched his chin with her finger. Just a simple touch and she made him burn. "You nicked yourself."

"I got distracted."

"What distracted you?"

"Thinking about last night when you had your mouth on my—"

She pressed the finger to his lips and glanced at the door. "Would you shush? Uncle Jack could be listening. For an old guy, he has extremely good hearing."

He nibbled on her finger and spoke in a hushed tone. "Then I guess we'll need to be extremely quiet." He reached for the button of her jeans, and her eyes widened.

"What are you doing?"

He flipped open the button and slid down her zipper. "What I've been fantasizing about doing ever since you started working here." He sent her an evil look. "Getting some hot cherry pie."

He didn't leave the kitchen until much later.

It turned out Gretchen had no trouble talking Uncle Jack into her plan. That very afternoon, they loaded up the bed of Wolfe's truck with pies. The first stop was Good Eats. Otis seemed to be at a loss for words when Uncle Jack shuffled in the door with Wolfe and Gretchen.

Thankfully, Thelma wasn't.

"Hello, y'all. What brings you in?"

"Uncle Jack wanted to stop by and give y'all a pie," Wolfe said.

Thelma's eyes widened. "Well . . . isn't that nice."

Uncle Jack thrust the pie at her. "It's not a big deal. I didn't make it. Gretchen did."

"Now don't be shy, Uncle Jack," Gretchen quickly said. "You helped me."

Uncle Jack snorted. "If you call me yakking while you bake help."

"That's how Thelma helps me," Otis said.

Thelma shot him an annoyed look as she took the pie. "Thank you so much, Uncle Jack." She glanced at Gretchen. "And you, Gretchen. I've heard all about your pies and can't wait to try them."

"It's blueberry," Uncle Jack said. "I heard Otis say once that it was his favorite."

Otis looked stunned. "It is."

Uncle Jack nodded. "Then there you go." He turned and headed for the door.

The rest of the deliveries went the same way. Uncle Jack wasn't exactly cordial, but he wasn't ornery either. Everyone who got a pie seemed to be stunned, which kept the conversation—and Jack saying something rude—to a minimum.

The last delivery was Kitty Carson. It took a while to find her on her route. Wolfe pulled up behind her postal truck and got a pie out of the bed while Gretchen helped Uncle Jack out of the backseat. They all three were waiting when Kitty came back to her truck. Her eyes widened when she saw them, but she recovered quickly.

"Well, hey, y'all. You want me to deliver that pie to someone? I don't have any shipping boxes that will fit it with me, but I have some at the post office that might work. Of course, if it's not local, that pie will be nothing but a bunch of crumbs by the time it arrives. Most postal workers aren't as careful as I am."

"I see you're just as talkative as you used to be," Uncle Jack said. "Your mama should've named you Chatty Cathy rather than Kitty." He shoved the pie at her. "We don't want it shipped. It's for you."

Kitty blinked and held a hand to her chest. "For me?"

"Ain't that what I just said?"

Kitty took the pie. "Thank you! I love pie." She glanced at Gretchen, and Wolfe could almost see her mind working. He was sure Kitty had heard about Gretchen leaving the ranch. He was also sure she would assume it had to do with the bathtub incident and she was right about Gretchen trying to seduce him. There was only one way he could think of to stop her from spreading that rumor.

He reached an arm around Gretchen and pulled her close. "Me and my woman are just helping Uncle Jack with his deliveries." He waited for Kitty to look surprised. But she didn't.

"I knew it!" She pumped her fist in the air. "After you defended her—and then hired her as your cook—I knew she meant more to you than the bubble bath hussy Sue Ann claimed she was. I told everyone, 'Wolfe Kingman has met his match. I guarantee it.'" She pressed a hand to her helmet hair and winked at Gretchen. "It's the red hair. Men can't resist us. Now I better get back to delivering the mail." Or more likely delivering the juicy bit of gossip Wolfe had just given her. "Thanks for the pie."

"You bet," Wolfe said. "If you like it, you be sure to stop by Nasty Jack's and we'll give you a slice on the house." He winked. "We need to keep our beautiful postal workers well fed."

Kitty blushed and pointed a finger at Gretchen. "You need to keep a close eye on this flirt, honey." Then she hustled back to her truck with the pie and zipped away.

When she was gone, Wolfe glanced over at Gretchen to see her staring at him with a stunned look. He figured he knew why. The term "my woman" was offensive to a lot of ladies and he shouldn't have used it. "I didn't mean any offense, Gretchen. It was just the easiest way to get the point across to Kitty without using a lot of words. It means you're mine, but not like a new truck or a pair of boots. I chose you, but you chose me too. Although I guess I should've asked if you choose me before I—"

Uncle Jack cut in with an exasperated snort. "I think what this boy is trying to tell you—and badly—is that, here in Texas, being a man's woman doesn't mean that you're his possession. It means you're his heart."

Damn if his uncle hadn't nailed it. Gretchen must have thought so too because she flung her arms around Wolfe and kissed him. When she finally drew back, he grinned. "I guess you don't mind being my woman."

She answered his smile with one of her own. "As long as you don't mind being my man."

"I wouldn't have it any other way, Red." He would've kissed her again if Uncle Jack hadn't butted in.

"If you two are done slobbering all over each other, I need to go home and take a nap. Being nice to people is tiring work."

# Chapter Seventeen

THE PIES WORKED.

On Taco Tuesday, Nasty Jack's was filled to overflowing with townsfolk. Gretchen could've kicked herself for not thinking about giving out pies sooner. Although maybe they shouldn't have given out so many pies. The bar was so busy she couldn't keep up. When Wolfe came in and gave her an order for ten tacos, and four slices of cherry and two slices of apple pie, she snapped at him.

"We're out of cherry! And apple! They get chess or blueberry or nothing!" She had just started filling taco shells when Wolfe came up behind her and pulled her into his arms. As much as she loved being in his arms, this was not the time for it.

"Stop." She tried to wiggle free. "I have to get these orders out, Wolfe."

He turned her around to face him. "Relax, Red. If people don't get their tacos and pie, they don't get their tacos and pie. It's not the end of the world."

"But they won't come back."

"They'll be back. Now that they realize Jack

isn't a villain, we won't be able to get rid of them." He smiled. "And you did it. You filled this bar to overflowing."

She shook her head. "Not me, my pies."

"And who made those pies and thought of the idea to deliver them to the townsfolk? Who softened up Uncle Jack and convinced him to deliver the pies with a semi-smile on his face?"

He had a good point, but she wasn't the only one responsible for the crowd outside the swinging doors. She cupped his face in her hands. "There wouldn't be a bar if not for you."

A look entered his eyes. A look that made her melt. "Then I guess we did it." He leaned in and kissed her. The kiss had just start to get heated when the doors swing open and Delaney stepped in.

"I'm all for kissing, but there's about to be a mutiny if you don't get those folks their pie."

Wolfe drew back and sighed. "We'll take this up later." He turned to Delaney. "Well, don't just stand there, sis. Help Gretchen make more pies."

She held up her hands. "Not me. I can't cook. But Lily and Stetson just showed up. I'll send Lily back." As she disappeared out the door, Wolfe turned to Gretchen.

"Stetson's here."

She smiled. "I told you he was ready to make up."

The door opened and Stetson and Lily walked into the kitchen. Gretchen worried there might be some tension between the two brothers. Especially if Stetson continued to be bossy. But he didn't act at all bossy. In fact, he immediately took the subservient role.

"Delaney says you need help." He grabbed two aprons off the hooks. He handed one to Lily and tied one around his waist before he turned to Wolfe. "What do you need me to do, little brother?"

The smile that spread over Wolfe's face made Gretchen's heart swell. It swelled even more as the night went on. Except for Adeline—who had decided to extend her trip to the Sagebrush Ranch, all the Kingmans showed up and helped. Stetson and Delaney took orders while Wolfe worked the bar and Buck bussed the tables. Mystic joined Lily and Gretchen in the kitchen. With Mystic dishing up tacos and Lily dishing up pie, Gretchen was able to make more pies and even take a break to peek out the door.

Everyone seemed to be having a good time. People were lined up at the bar, chatting with Wolfe as he mixed drinks and filled glasses with beer. Other folks were sitting at tables, enjoying pie and tacos. The dance floor was full of two-steppers dancing to an Alan Jackson song playing on the jukebox.

Gretchen glanced over to Uncle Jack's table, wanting to see how he was taking the night's success. But Uncle Jack wasn't enjoying the crowd in his bar. It looked like he had fallen asleep. He was slumped in his chair with his arms hanging at his sides. She might've smiled at the man being able to sleep with all the noise if she hadn't noticed the odd angle of his head and the pale color of his skin.

She quickly pushed out the doors and headed over to the table.

"Uncle Jack?" When he didn't respond, she grabbed his arm and gently shook him. "Wake up, Uncle Jack." But he didn't wake up. Fear consumed her. She turned and raced back to the bar.

"Wolfe!"

He glanced up and must have read her panic because he hurried out from behind the bar. "What is it? What happened?"

"Your uncle. Something's wrong. He won't wake up."

"Stet! Call 911!" Wolfe yelled as he hurried over to his uncle's table. He carefully lifted him out of the chair and placed him on the floor. He checked his mouth for any obstructions before he started doing chest compressions. Gretchen watched with her hands clutched to her chest as Buck and Delaney herded everyone out of the bar.

By the time the paramedics got there, it was just Gretchen, Mystic, and the Kingmans watching Wolfe's desperate attempts to save Uncle Jack. Stetson had tried to take over, but Wolfe had refused. He even refused help from the paramedics.

"You can stop now, sir. We got this." A paramedic took Wolfe's arm, but he shook it off.

"Don't fuckin' touch me! I'm not done." He thumped Uncle Jack's chest. "Come on, you mean old sonofabitch, don't you die on me."

Tears dripped down Gretchen's cheeks as Stetson and Buck took Wolfe's arms and pulled him away. But he even fought his brothers.

"Let me go! Let me help him."

"You've done all you can do, Wolfe," Stetson said. "Believe me, you've done all you can do."

The tortured sound that came from Wolfe's throat cracked Gretchen's heart right in two. He jerked free from his brothers. But he didn't go back to where the paramedics were working on Uncle Jack. Instead, he headed for the door.

Gretchen started after him, but Stetson caught her arm. "Let him go, Gretchen. He needs some time."

Delaney put an arm around her. "He'll be okay, Gretch. Wolfe's tough."

But Delaney was wrong. Gretchen knew that inside the tough bad boy was a tender heart easily bruised.

Once Uncle Jack was loaded in the ambulance and on his way to the hospital, Lily turned to Gretchen. "You can ride with us to the hospital."

She shook her head. "I think I'll stay here in case Wolfe comes back."

Lily nodded and gave her a hug. "We'll keep you posted on Uncle Jack."

After everyone left, Gretchen cleaned up the bar area before she headed to the kitchen to put away the leftovers and wash the dishes. She was at the sink scouring a pan when she heard a loud crash come from the bar. She dried her hands and hurried out to see Wolfe smashing Uncle Jack's table with a chair. Both the table and the chair were nothing but a pile of splinter wood by the time he finished.

He tossed the chair leg he still held in his hand across the room before he turned and saw her standing there. He looked like he'd been in a fight. He had a cut above his left eye and the eye looked red and swollen.

"What are you still doing here?" he growled.

She went to the bar and filled a dishtowel with ice and brought it back to him, but he refused to accept it. "I'm fine. Just fuckin' fine." He hesitated as if he hated to ask the next question. "How's Uncle Jack?"

She wanted to tell him that his uncle would be okay. But she couldn't lie. Jack was over eighty. Whether it was a stroke or a heart attack, his chances of surviving were slim. "He was still alive when they took him away."

Wolfe moved behind the bar and grabbed a bottle of whiskey and opened it. Instead of pouring it in a glass, he took a deep pull right out of the bottle before he slammed it back down on the bar. He stood there with his hands resting on the edge of the bar and his head hanging between his shoulders. She wanted to comfort him but she knew he was feeling too raw to be touched. So she sat down at the bar and waited.

Finally he spoke.

"Everyone thinks the Kingmans are so blessed. But we're as cursed as this town." He glanced over at her. "Did you know that not one of my male relatives on my father's side lived past the age of sixty-five? Not one. Except Uncle Jack. And now even he is living on borrowed time."

"But aren't we all just living on borrowed time? Which is why we have to live and love as much as we can while we're here."

She knew she had said the wrong thing when his face contorted with hurt and pain. He picked up the bottle and threw it against the wall. "Love. I hate the fuckin' word!"

"No you don't. You're just hurting right now."

He slammed a fist on the bar. "You're damn right I'm hurting and I'm tired of feeling this pain. Do you hear me? I'm tired of everyone I love dying on me. And the last thing I need right now is you standing there looking at me like that."

"Like what?"

"Like I'm something special."

"You are special."

"No." He shook his head. "I'm not anything special. So get that out of your head right now. I'm a womanizing bad boy who wants nothing to do with love and all the pain that goes with it. I told you I could give you more. But sadly, I didn't realize that I don't have any more to give. I've got nothing for you, Gretchen. Nothing. One day, you'll meet someone who is special, and you'll thank your lucky stars that you didn't let some empty promise ruin a lifetime of happiness. Now get out of here. Do you hear me? Get out of here and never look back."

He moved from behind the bar and headed for the stairs.

Gretchen should have done what he asked. He'd made his feelings perfectly clear. He didn't want love. And she couldn't stay with a man who refused to love like her mama. But she couldn't leave him either. She couldn't leave him when he was hurting so badly. It would probably be a mistake she would pay for later. But after she locked the doors and turned off the lights, she followed him up the stairs.

She found him in Uncle Jack's room. He'd taken off his boots and was lying on the bed staring up at the ceiling. She didn't say anything. She just turned off the lights and climbed into the bed next to him.

"You don't listen very well. I don't want you here."

"So I heard." She placed her arms around him and rested her head on his chest. She had to wonder if she was doing this for Wolfe or for herself. This would be the last time she got to hold him. To breathe in his scent. To hear his heart thump against her ear. To feel the heat of his hard body.

Tears filled her eyes and rolled down her cheeks. She cried. She cried for Uncle Jack. And for Wolfe. And for her mama . . . and for herself. She cried even more when Wolfe's arms came around her and he brushed a kiss over the top of her head.

"Shh, baby. Please don't cry."

But she couldn't seem to stop. He lifted her chin and kissed the tears from her cheeks. "Please, Red. Please stop." He kissed his way to her lips. The heat of his mouth on hers caused them both to draw back. They stared at each other for only a moment before they came together again.

It was like coming home. Their lips and tongues welcomed each other in a frenzied greeting that left them both breathless. Their movements became frenzied as they tugged off clothes in a rush to get to bare skin. Once nothing was between them, it was like a switch was flipped. Their kisses became slower. Deeper. Their touches longer. More intense. Maybe it was because they both knew this would be the last time that each kiss and caress became something unto itself.

When Wolfe finally entered her, he moved in slow, deep strokes that fanned the heat of her desire like a soft breeze fanning a flame. Their eyes remained locked as he held himself above her and guided her toward orgasm. Her climax was as long and intense as their lovemaking had been. It crested and then held her aloft as Wolfe reached his.

His gaze never left her as he moaned and trembled his release. She saw something in his eyes. Something that said this hadn't just been sex. But before she could be sure, his eyelids closed. A tear leaked out of the corner and rolled down his cheek. Then another. And another. Without saying a word, she pulled him into her arms and held him close as he wept.

A short time later, he fell asleep. She listened to his even breathing for a long time before she scooted out from under him and got dressed. Before she left, she pulled the blanket at the end of the bed over him and pressed a kiss to his forehead.

"I love you, Wolfe Kingman."

## Chapter Eighteen

WOLFE WOKE UP hurting. His head hurt. His face hurt. But mostly his heart hurt. The hurt only intensified when he opened his eyes and saw he was alone. He listened for any sound that would prove Gretchen hadn't left, but all he heard was his own shallow breathing.

And what did he expect? He'd asked her to leave, and he'd gotten his wish. His brain knew it was for the best. She didn't need someone like him. She needed someone who could love her unconditionally. Someone who wasn't terrified of loving and losing. That wasn't him. He didn't want to add another person to the people he loved. He couldn't live through this pain again. He damn well couldn't.

He sat up and glanced around the room. Everything was how his uncle had left it. His worn western shirts hung in the closet. His tattered slippers sat on the floor beneath. The chair where he liked to read the newspaper sat in one corner. A five-drawer dresser in the other. On the dresser was an ornate, ivory-inlaid box. Wolfe had once asked Uncle Jack where he'd gotten it and Jack had told him it was none of his damn business.

Wolfe should've stayed out of Uncle Jack's business. He shouldn't have tried to help. He shouldn't have hired Gretchen. He certainly shouldn't have made love to her. He should've guarded his heart like he'd always done. If he had, he wouldn't be sitting here hurting.

But he knew how to stop the hurting. All he had to do was what he'd done before. All he had to do was put Jasper and Uncle Jack and Gretchen in the same vault where he'd kept his mother and father. Once they were locked in there tight, he could move on and be the same carefree Wolfe he'd always been.

But first he had to leave Nasty Jack's and never come back. There were too many memories here. Memories of Jasper smiling as he poured drinks. Memories of Uncle Jack yelling orders from across the bar. Memories of Gretchen in the kitchen baking pies . . . in this bed holding him tight.

A spear of pain punched him hard in the chest, but he ignored it and got up and got dressed. He went to his room and packed his bags, then started for the stairs. He stopped halfway down, retraced his steps, and grabbed the ivory box from Jack's dresser.

As soon as he drove under the Kingman Ranch entrance sign with its two rearing stallions, he expected the pain in his heart to ease. It didn't. In fact, it seemed to intensify. Images of Gretchen filled his head: sitting in a tub of bubbles, lying on top of him in the laundry room, riding a horse next to him with tears in her eyes.

Instead of parking at the house, he drove to the stables. Thankfully, Tab was nowhere around. Wolfe didn't feel like talking to anyone. When he stepped into Mutt's stall, the horse seemed to sense what he needed and came over to offer his love.

Just like Gretchen.

She had never expected anything from him. She just gave him what he'd needed—even after he'd hurt her with his words. She loved him. He'd felt her love like a soothing balm as she held him while he cried. But it was better to hurt her a little now, than hurt her more when she found out he could never give her what she wanted. What she deserved.

The spear of pain came again. This time sharper. Deeper. He led Mutt out of the stall and quickly saddled him. As soon as they were out of the stable yard, he gave Mutt free rein. Maybe if he ran long enough and fast enough, he could outrun the pain. But it only grew worse the faster Mutt ran.

Realizing he was taking his pain out on Mutt, Wolfe reined him in. When he saw where they had stopped, he wanted to shake his fist at the overcast sky. Only divine intervention would have brought him to the Kingman family cemetery.

His first thought was to spur Mutt into another run and get the hell out of there. But the horse was lathered and winded and needed a break. Wolfe dismounted and tied him to a maple before he turned to the cemetery.

All the Kingmans were buried here, along with a few champion horses. As a kid, Wolfe had spent a lot of time at his mother's grave. He'd thought that maybe she would impart words of wisdom to him from beyond. She hadn't. After his father died, Wolfe had been pissed at God and hadn't come back to the graveyard. He'd hoped if he didn't acknowledge death, it would leave him alone. If he just concentrated on living and having fun, the grim reaper would pass him by. But it seemed that death came to you whether you acknowledged it or not.

The cemetery gate stuck and he had to kick it to gain entry. Once inside, he walked down the rows of his ancestors and looked at the tombstones dating all the way back to the eighteen hundreds. Most he'd never known. Some he'd met but couldn't remember.

Like Grandpa King.

He stopped at the huge marble headstone with an image of Kingman castle carved into it, along with the words, *"I came from the land and to the land I return."* To the left of King's headstone were Wolfe's father's and mother's headstones. His mother's had her name, the dates spanning her life, and *Beloved Wife and Mother*. His father's had only his name and the dates.

"I didn't know what to put on Daddy's."

Wolfe turned to see Stetson standing by the gate. His brother looked as tired as Wolfe felt. He had no trouble opening the gate. But Stetson never had trouble with anything . . . while Wolfe seemed to struggle with everything.

Stetson must've read the pain on his face because he rested a hand on Wolfe's shoulder. "Are you okay?"

Normally, Wolfe would've pretended. He couldn't today.

He shook his head.

Stetson's hand tightened as he nodded. "Yeah, it's been a tough night. But Uncle Jack is hanging in there. The ornery cuss might just make it." He released Wolfe's shoulder and looked at their daddy's headstone. "I wish I had put something better on it. It would've been a lie to put loving husband, but I could've put loving father. Daddy loved us. He just wasn't good at showing it."

"Something that runs in the family," Wolfe muttered.

"You're right," Stetson said. "I have never been good at showing my feelings. And I'm sorry. I know it was hard on you not having a mama or a devoted daddy. All you had was an inept brother who thought issuing orders was the way to get his siblings to turn out right."

"You weren't even out of college, Stet. You did the best you could. And I wasn't talking about you. I was talking about me. I'm the one who struggles to show people I love them."

Stetson sighed. "I used to believe that. But someone pointed out the truth to me. Out of all of us, you show your love the most, Wolfe. Maybe not with words, but with actions. Look what you did for Uncle Jack. You showed him love—showed him that there is something much more important than land and money." He hesitated for just a second before he pulled Wolfe into his arms. "I love you, brother. And I'm damn proud of the man you've become."

Wolfe wrapped his arms around Stetson and buried his face in his neck, releasing his pain. "I can't lose any more people, Stet. I just can't."

Stetson's arms tightened. "I know."

They stood there holding tight to one another for a long time before Stetson drew back. "Come on. I want to show you something."

He led Wolfe around to the other side of King's gravestone to a headstone that looked brand new. *Jasper Daniel Kingman, Beloved Grandson and Cousin, "He always had a beer and a smile for everyone."*

Wolfe smiled. "It's true."

"Then let's remember that and forget the rest," Stetson said. "We might not know why Jasper did what he did. And we don't know what happened between Uncle Jack and King. But family is family. Regardless of what happens, we, ultimately, belong together. The Kingman Ranch is your home, Wolfe."

Wolfe nodded. "I'm ready to come home."

It was the truth. There was no reason for him to go back to the bar. Uncle Jack was gone . . . and so was Gretchen.

Stetson thumped him on the back. "Then let's get to the house. On the way, you can show me what that ugly mutt of a horse can do. Delaney is convinced he's the best cutting horse she's ever seen."

Mutt was more than happy to show off his cutting skills for Stetson when they stopped by a herd of cattle in the east pasture. As they raced back to the house, Mutt beat out Stetson' thoroughbred by a full length.

Once they arrived at the stables, Stetson dismounted and came over to praise Mutt. "You might not look like much, you mangy animal, but you sure proved me wrong."

Mutt drew back his lips and grinned.

Everyone was waiting in the kitchen when Stetson and Wolfe walked in the back door. Including Adeline and Gage. Adeline immediately got up from the table and hugged Wolfe tight.

"I'm so sorry to hear about Uncle Jack. I know how close you two have become. I'm praying he'll pull through." She drew back and glanced behind him. "Where's Gretchen?"

Wolfe couldn't talk about Gretchen. His emotions were still too raw. "I don't know. Look, it's been a long night. So I think I'm going to go upstairs and get some rest before I head to the hospital."

He should've known Adeline wouldn't let him get away so easily. He had no more than stepped inside his bedroom when she followed him in.

"What happened, Wolfe?"

"I don't want to talk about it, Addie."

She closed the door behind her. "Well, I do. And I'm not leaving until you tell me what happened to Gretchen."

"Nothing happened to Gretchen."

"Then why isn't she here?"

He sat down on the bed and tugged off his boots. "I don't know how you can ask that when you were the one who told Stetson not to hire her back. If she'd stayed on the ranch, maybe . . ."

Adeline finished the sentence for him. "You wouldn't have fallen in love with her?" When he sent her a startled look, she laughed. "Don't tell me that you don't know, little brother."

He knew. He just didn't want to hear the words out loud. They struck his already bruised heart like arrows. But his sister's next words distracted him from the pain.

"I could tell you were falling for Gretchen when we spoke on the phone." Adeline sat down on the bed next to him. "Which is why I didn't want Stetson rehiring her. And why I asked you to make sure she didn't leave. I hoped the time together would help you figure out your feelings."

His boot slipped from his fingers. "You planned it all?"

"Of course not. I didn't plan on her mother showing up or Gretchen leaving the ranch." She smiled. "But it certainly fit nicely with my plans to get you two together." Her smile faded. "Now what did you do to wreck it? Please don't tell me you broke her heart."

"That's the last thing I want to do. Which is why I broke it off with her. Gretchen is special. She deserves better than me."

He expected a little sympathy for the sacrifice he was making. Instead, his sweet oldest sister punched him right in the arm. Not a little tap, but a full-out punch that hurt like hell. He grabbed his arm and glared at her.

"What the hell, Addie?"

She rubbed her fist. "If that hadn't hurt so bad, I'd hit you again. Maybe it would knock some sense into you. Gage tried to pull that same you-deserve-better bit with me. That's like breaking up with someone and saying 'It's not you, it's me.' If you're going to break up with someone, give it to them straight. Don't make up some cock-and-bull excuse for why you don't deserve them. Man up, Wolfe. If you love someone, you'll do whatever it takes to deserve them. Do you love Gretchen?" When he didn't answer her, she shoved him, almost knocking him off the bed. "Do you love Gretchen?"

"Yes! I love her! But I refuse to love another person and lose them. I'm not that strong, Addie. I'm just not that strong."

Adeline's eyes softened. "Oh, Wolfe. I know you've lost a lot of loved ones. We all have. Yes, it's painful and devastating. But you know what's even more devastating? A loveless life. Look at Jasper. He pushed love away and hate consumed him. If he had just accepted the love people offered, maybe he wouldn't have become so bitter and unhappy. He might not have owned a share of the ranch, but he was part of our family—part of the town. And he threw it all away. When people offer us love, it's not about whether we're worthy. It's about accepting that love and loving back. You've always acted so tough. But I know the soft heart beneath. Gretchen sees it too.

That's why she fell for you." She smiled. "Looking back, I think she fell for you the second she saw you. Which explains why she was so klutzy around you."

"She's not a klutz. She was just working at job she wasn't suited for. You should see her in a kitchen."

Adeline smiled. "I look forward to it. Bring her home, little brother. She's a good-hearted woman and she deserves a good-hearted man. You can be that man, Wolfe. All you have to do is take a chance."

## Chapter Nineteen

Gretchen thought she would wake up feeling as heartsick as she had the night before. And her heart did feel bruised. But somewhere during the night, she had come to terms with the fact that Wolfe could never love her like she deserved to be loved. As she stared at the sun shining in through the high windows, she realized she wasn't scared of love anymore. It hurt, but it also healed.

She would never regret loving Wolfe. Never.

He had made her look in the mirror and see herself as something other than a fat, clumsy, freckle-faced woman. He had made her realize she was beautiful and desirable. Funny and kind. Strong and powerful. And worthy of love. Even if he wasn't the man to give it to her. And maybe she wouldn't find any man to give it to her. But that was okay too. She didn't need Mr. Right to be happy.

Sitting up, she reached for her cellphone and called the hospital to check on Uncle Jack. Because she wasn't immediate family, they refused to tell her anything except that he was still in intensive care. At least he was still alive. After she hung up, she prayed for his full recovery.

Once she'd showered, she got dressed in jeans and the cowboy boots Delaney had given her before she fixed her hair like Mystic had shown her.

She would miss both women. But not as much as she missed Adeline. If she had ever needed her friend, she needed her now. But talking to Addie would only weaken her resolve to leave. She had to go. Regardless of how confident she felt this morning, she knew she couldn't live anywhere near Wolfe without following him around like a lovesick puppy.

After she finished with her hair, she started to pack. There was little to pack. She no longer wanted her housekeeping dresses. Her mother was right. They did look like she had bought them at an Amish yard sale. She left them in a neat stack on the bed and would ask Mystic to give them to charity. When she had packed everything she wanted to keep, she closed her suitcase, took one last look at the bed where she had spent an amazing night with Wolfe, and headed out the door.

As she was putting her suitcase in the trunk of her car, Hester's voice rang out.

"Running away?"

She turned to see the older woman sitting on the porch, rocking slowly and stroking the crystal that hung around her neck. Gretchen slammed the trunk closed and walked toward the house. "I was planning on coming to say goodbye to you and Mystic." She climbed the steps. "Thank you so much for giving me a place to stay and making me feel like family. How much do I owe you?"

"We'll settle up in a minute. Right now, you need to sit down and tell me why you're leaving when your true love is right here in Cursed."

Gretchen sat down in the chair next to Hester's and smiled sadly. "Because sometimes true love isn't enough."

Hester snorted. "Those are the exact words your mama used."

"My mama? When did you meet my mama?"

"She stopped in here on her way out of town and wanted me to read her palm and tell her if she was ever going to find the perfect man."

It wasn't surprising. Her mama had always loved psychics and had wasted a lot of money calling the 1-900 numbers to get help in her search for love. "And what did you tell her?" Gretchen asked.

"The truth. There's no such thing as a perfect man—or a perfect woman. All human beings are flawed. And yet, most people still think they're going to find that one person who makes all their dreams come true. That one person who will make their life easy. But life isn't easy. And neither is love. To be happy in both, you have to work for it. Not run away when the going gets tough."

"I bet my mother didn't take that well."

"It's hard to see your own mistakes. It's much easier to see other people's." Hester's piercing eyes seemed to drill right through her. "And it looks like the apple doesn't fall far from the tree."

She stared at Hester. "What do you mean? I'm not like my mama. She never gave men a chance to love her."

Hester cocked an eyebrow. "And you have?"

Tears filled Gretchen's eyes. "Wolfe doesn't want to be in love."

"Well, of course he doesn't. It hurts like hell to lose the ones you love, and Wolfe has lost a lot of people he's loved. He doesn't want to feel that pain again. He doesn't realize it's too late. He already loves you."

It was pathetic how quickly Gretchen latched onto Hester's words. "You've seen that? Wolfe loves me?"

Hester shook her head. "I don't read people's feelings. That's Mystic's gift. But I've seen Wolfe's struggle to find his place in his family and in this town. And I saw how happy he was the morning he snuck out of your room—like he'd found that place. I don't know what went on between the two of you, but I do know running away isn't going to fix it. After watching your mama, you should know better."

The truth of Hester's words hit Gretchen like an anvil falling from the sky. She had hated her mama packing up and leaving whenever things didn't go exactly how she wanted them to. And yet that was exactly what Gretchen was doing.

She *was* running.

"You're right," she whispered. "I am like my mama—finding any excuse to leave because I'm too scared to stay and fight for the love I want." She got up. "Keep my room, Ms. Malone."

Hester rubbed her crystal and smiled. "There's no need for that. You won't be back. The Kingman Ranch is where you belong. Now go get your man." She glanced up at the sky. "But you'll need something first." She went inside the house and returned with a red rain slicker. "A storm is coming."

Hester was right. By the time Gretchen got to the Kingman Ranch, the sun had been completely obliterated by dark clouds and it was raining cats and dogs. But the rain didn't make her homecoming any less sweet. As soon as the castle came into view, a big ball of joy burst inside of Gretchen. Without hesitation, she parked around back, jumped out, and raced for the back door.

She froze when she saw all the Kingmans, except for Wolfe, sitting at the kitchen table. "Oh, pardon me. I hate to interrupt your breakfast, but I need to talk to—"

"You're not interrupting anything." Adeline got up from the table and rushed over to give Gretchen a hug. "I'm so glad you're still here. I was worried Hester wouldn't be able to keep you in town."

"You called Hester?"

Adeline smiled. "I didn't. Wolfe did. He didn't want you go anywhere until he could figure out a plan."

"A plan? A plan for what?"

Before Adeline could answer, Delaney spoke. "To get you to forgive him for being an idiot. Stetson thought he should just drive into town and ask your forgiveness. Adeline thought he should plan a romantic dinner in the labyrinth. And Buck thought he should ride into town on a white horse." She shot an annoyed look over at her brother. "As if a woman needs a knight coming to her rescue."

"It was better than your idea of him sending her a text that said, 'I'm sorry. Kingman men are known to be arrogant idiots. It's in their DNA.'"

Delaney shrugged. "Well, it is."

Gretchen was too stunned to say anything. The fact that Wolfe was sorry and wanted to make it up to her had a warm glow settling in her stomach and a smile blooming on her face.

Stetson winked at her. "It looks like all our advice wasn't needed. Go on up, Gretchen. He's in his room."

Gretchen turned and hurried up the stairs. She tapped lightly on the door. When he didn't answer, she opened it and peeked in. Wolfe wasn't there, but the bathroom door was closed and she could hear water running. She smiled. It seemed fitting that she should walk in on Wolfe while he was showering. Except when she opened the bathroom door, she didn't find him in the shower.

She found him sitting in the huge bathtub surrounded by bubbles.

When he saw her, his eyes widened.

"Little Red Riding Hood?"

In her need to find him, she'd forgotten all about wearing the red rain poncho Hester had given her. She pushed back the hood and moved closer to the bathtub.

"The Big Bad Wolfe, I presume. Although the bubbles take a little away from your badness."

He smiled. "I was hoping for a grander grand

gesture, but it was all I could come up with on short notice."

"I guess Hester called to say I was on my way."

He nodded and his eyes softened. "I'm so sorry, Red. I didn't mean what I said last night. I was just upset over Uncle Jack and I took it out on you. Please don't leave—"

She held a finger to her lips. "Shhh. You're ruining my fantasy." She removed the slicker and dropped it to the floor, then pulled off her shirt.

His gaze lowered. "Your fantasy?"

She reached behind her and unclasped her bra, allowing it to join her shirt as she toed off her boots. "Yes, my fantasy. The one I've had stuck in my head ever since walking in on you taking a shower. The fantasy where I'm brave enough to strip naked and join you. And don't ruin it for me by talking about things that don't matter. I'm here." She reached for the button of her jeans. "And I'm not going anywhere."

When she was completely naked, she stepped into the tub and eased down into bubbles. She didn't know if it was the heat of the water or the heat of Wolfe's body that had her sighing with contentment as she adjusted her legs on either side of his. Once she was comfortable, she hooked her arms around his broad shoulders and kissed him. It was a perfect kiss. Soft and lush and filled with emotion that spoke much louder than words. And still, when she finally drew back, she couldn't help saying them.

"I love you."

She didn't expect him to start singing hallelujahs, but she didn't expect him to get mad either.

"Dammit, Red. You should've slapped me or punched me or ranted and raved and told me what a jerk I've been. Instead, you bring me to my knees by forgiving me and telling me that you love me." His eyes misted over. "I don't deserve you, Gretchen Flaherty. I damn well don't deserve you." He pulled her onto his lap. "But I'm not about to let you get away. My life had no meaning until you showed up. I was just going through the motions trying to shield myself from any kind of feelings that would cause me pain. And then this beautiful angel in an apron arrived and turned my world upside down. You made me feel things I didn't want to feel. Which is why I fought so hard against loving you."

He smoothed a strand of her hair back from her face. "But you're impossible not to love, Red. How can you not love a person who sees each day as a gift you need to enjoy and not waste? A person who puts everyone else's needs before her own? A person who loves so completely without any hesitation or restrictions? I love you, Red. I love you so much I was terrified of losing you. I'm still terrified."

Gretchen's heart swelled to bursting and tears of joy rolled down her cheeks. "You aren't going to lose me, Wolfe Kingman. Haven't you figured that out by now? I'm like a turnip. I always turn-up when you least expect it."

He tipped back his head and laughed. She joined him. There was nothing that made her happier than making a wolf laugh. When they sobered, his eyes grew serious.

"Let's do it."

"I'm sitting on your lap with my legs wrapped around your waist. I thought that was a forgone conclusion."

"I wasn't talking about sex, sweetheart. Although I plan to do that too—a lot. I was talking about getting married."

Her eyes widened. "But I thought you didn't want to get married."

"That was before I met a redheaded, green-eyed beauty who stole my heart. Now I can't wait to be shackled to you. Anything to keep you right by my side." He tipped up her chin and looked into her eyes. "You're not your mother, Gretchen. And I'm not my father. I'm going to spend the rest of my life proving to you that you made the right choice. That I'm Mr. Right."

Gretchen had once thought she could do quite nicely without ever finding her Mr. Right. And she probably would have. But as she stared into Wolfe's beloved gray eyes, she realized there was a big difference between doing quite nicely and living happily ever after.

She cradled his face in her hands. "As my mama always says, 'Yes, I'll marry you.'" Wolfe went to kiss her, but she held back. "No big wedding. I just want something small with no chicken dancing."

"No big wedding. I promise." He leaned in and whispered against her lips. "Now about that fantasy. Why don't you give me a rundown so I know what part to play."

She smiled. "You know what part. Devour me, Wolfe."

And he did.

# Chapter Twenty

"I DIDN'T THINK I'D ever see the day that my bad boy big brother got married."

Wolfe turned from the mirror and saw Delaney standing in the doorway of his bedroom looking stunning in a red saloon girl costume.

"Excuse me, miss," he said teasingly. "But have you seen my little sister? Braids, old jeans, and crap-covered cowboy boots."

She placed a hand on her hip and scowled at him. "Very funny. It wasn't my idea for the bride and her attendants to dress up like saloon girl hookers. I thought we should all go as old movie or television cowboys too, but Addie, Gretchen, and Mystic vetoed the idea." She walked in and flopped down on his bed. "What was Addie thinking combining your wedding with the Cowboy Ball, anyway? And why does the ball have to be here at our house? Why couldn't it still be at the church gymnasium where everyone got to dress in normal clothing? Then I wouldn't be trussed up in a corset that won't even let me take a breath."

Wolfe laughed and went back to tying the red

bandana around his neck. "It's not that bad, Del."

"You won't be thinking that when I faint during the wedding ceremony."

"You won't faint. And it wasn't Addie's idea to change the ball to a costume ball, it was the Ladies' Auxiliary Club's. They all thought it would be fun to dress up in old western costumes. What better place to hold a western ball than in a western castle?"

Delaney blew out her breath. "But did she have to combine it with your wedding? If she hadn't, I would be Calamity Jane right now with a couple of six-shooters."

"It wasn't Addie's idea to combine the wedding with the ball. It was mine. Gretchen has already had to endure too many wedding receptions. This way, she gets a big party with all her friends and family without any bad memories."

In the reflection of the mirror, he saw Delaney squint at him. "Talk about imposters? Where did my insensitive bad boy brother go?"

He finished adjusting the bandana before he turned. "He fell in love. You should try it."

She shook her head and the mass of dark curls on the top of her head shifted precariously. "Not me. No man is going to change me. I plan to sow my wild oats just like you did. Then maybe I'll think about getting married." She got up. "Now I need to go check to see if Uncle Jack is almost ready so I can report back to Addie." She shook her head. "Our big sister has become as controlling as Stetson since she got pregnant." She strode out of the room.

When she was gone, Wolfe turned back to the mirror. He'd been going for the John Wayne look. But even with the double-breasted shirt and bandana, he looked nothing like "The Duke." He probably would have been better off going as an outlaw. But it was too late now. He went to pick up his beige felt hat sitting on the dresser and noticed Uncle Jack's ivory inlaid box.

Once Uncle Jack had recovered from his heart attack, Wolfe had tried to give the box back to him. But Jack had told him to keep it. For some reason, Wolfe hadn't opened it yet. Maybe because he was scared at what he'd find. He didn't want to find proof Uncle Jack had been conspiring with Jasper.

But when he opened the box, he didn't find anything but photographs. There were old ones of Uncle Jack and Aunt Mary's wedding and numerous ones of them with their son. Jack Junior had looked a lot like Stetson. Tall, broad shouldered, and somber. He hadn't looked anything like Jasper. Wolfe's heart tightened when he came to the picture of Jasper standing behind the bar with a bright smile on his face. To Wolfe, Jasper would always be this man. His outgoing, friendly cousin. His beloved friend.

He started to put the photos back in the box when he noticed the folded piece of paper at the bottom. He took it out and opened it.

*I, John Nathanial Kingman, leave my bar, Nasty Jack's, and everything I own to my great-nephew, Wolfgang Rudolph Kingman.*

Since his uncle hadn't had possession of the

box, he would've had to write the will before his heart attack.

Wolfe's eyes welled with tears.

"You ready?"

He turned to see his best man standing in the doorway. Unlike Wolfe, Stetson looked exactly like John Wayne. He even had the swagger as he walked into the room and looked down at the paper in Wolfe's hand.

"What's that?"

"Uncle Jack's will. He wants me to have the bar."

Stetson tipped his head. "I don't know why you look so surprised. You're the only one who stepped up to the plate to help him when he needed it. He knows you'll keep the bar and his legacy going."

"But I'm not a bar owner. I'm a rancher." He folded the will and placed it back in the box. When he turned around, he found Stetson smiling.

"From what I've seen, you're both."

Wolfe had never thought his brother would praise him for working the ranch. Or running a bar. But in the last few months, things had changed between them. They still argued and rarely saw eye to eye, but they had learned to accept their differences—as if there was an unspoken oath between them to never end up like King and Jack.

"So you wouldn't mind me owning a bar?" he asked.

Stetson shrugged. "As long as your brother gets

free drinks and pie. Now come on. It's time." He hesitated. "You're not having second thoughts, are you?"

A few months ago, he'd been dead set against marriage. Now he had no reservations at all. He grabbed his hat and pulled it on. "Not one."

"Good. Because Adeline told me if you were, I was to knock you out and drag you to the garden."

Wolfe halted on his way out the door. "You think you can knock me out, Duke?"

"I know it, Duke. But the proof will have to wait for another day." Stetson hooked an arm over Wolfe's shoulders. "Let's get you hitched, little bro."

From the time Gretchen appeared on Uncle Jack's arm, everything became a blur but her. Her strawberry blond hair was fixed just the way he liked it, falling around her shoulders in an array of curls. In the beautiful green saloon girl costume that brought out her eyes, she looked breathtaking in the Texas sun that was setting behind her.

But what really took his breath away was the love he saw on her face. When she and Uncle Jack reached him, he couldn't help taking her hand and holding on tight while Reverend Ransom spoke to Uncle Jack.

"Who gives this woman to be married to this man?"

"Well, I was supposed to," Uncle Jack grumbled. "But as you can see, my nephew just took without me giving. It runs in his family." He pointed a gnarled finger at Wolfe. "She's a keeper. Don't screw it up." He glanced around. "Well, where's my seat?"

Adeline hurried over and took his arm. At six months pregnant, Addie's saloon girl dress didn't fit quite as well as Mystic, Delaney, and Gretchen's. She still looked beautiful. Gage, who was dressed like the Sundance Kid, couldn't keep his eyes off her as she directed Uncle Jack to a chair before coming back to stand next to Gretchen.

After the vows were spoken, Wolfe finally got to do what he'd been wanting to do ever since his bride had reached him. He kissed her. He kissed her with all the love in his heart. He would've gone on kissing her if Reverend Ransom hadn't cleared his throat. Wolfe begrudgingly drew away. But when he opened his eyes to see Gretchen looking at him with such longing, he didn't care what the preacher or anyone else thought. He wanted to kiss her again . . . but in private.

Before Reverend Ransom had even pronounced them man and wife, he took Gretchen's hand and headed for the castle. Unfortunately, Adeline stepped in front of them.

"Just where do you think you're going?"

"You need to move, Addie," he said. "I know the guests for the Cowboy Ball will be arriving any second and you want the newly wedded couple there to greet them, but I need to talk to Gretchen privately for a few minutes."

"Talk?" Adeline rolled her eyes. "As if I'd believe that. You two can't keep your hands off each other since you both moved back to the ranch."

It was the truth. If Wolfe wasn't sneaking into Gretchen's room, she was sneaking into his. Their trysts weren't just kept to nighttime. During the day, they'd enjoyed the barn and the stables . . . and the kitchen. Just thinking about those enjoyable memories had Wolfe pleading.

"Please, Addie."

Adeline crossed her arms. "You can't take Gretchen back to the castle when it's overrun with caterers and the guests will be arriving soon. Now the labyrinth, on the other hand, will be nice and quiet and perfect for . . . talking. But you only get an hour before I'm going to come looking for you. I want to celebrate my little brother marrying my best friend." She gave Gretchen a tight hug. "I'm so happy for you."

"Thank you, Addie," Gretchen said. "Thank you for being the best friend a girl could ask for."

Adeline drew back. "We're not just friends, Gretchen. We're sisters."

They both got teary eyed, and Wolfe figured he'd better get Gretchen out of there before the waterworks started. She released a startled gasp when he scooped her up in his arms and started for the stairs that led to the labyrinth. But then she looped her arms around his neck and settled against him with a satisfied sigh.

"Happy?" he asked.

"That doesn't even come close to describing how I feel."

He knew exactly how she felt. He drew her closer as they entered the hedge maze. It was the one place he'd yet to bring Gretchen. When he stepped through the break in the hedge that led to the secret garden, he said a silent thank you to his big sister for making this moment so special.

At least a dozen lit candles surrounded the edge of the fountain, their flickering light reflecting off the water that flowed from the top tier. Along with the candles was an ice bucket with champagne and two fluted glasses. On the lawn next to it, a blanket had been spread out and covered with colorful pillows.

"Oh, my," Gretchen said as he set her on her feet. "This is beautiful."

He pulled her back into his arms and kissed her. "You're beautiful."

She smiled up at him. "Thank you." It did his heart good that she no longer doubted her beauty or tried to deny it. "You're beautiful too, husband."

"Husband." He sighed. "I never thought I'd think that word was the most wonderful word in the dictionary. Although its not as wonderful as 'wife.'" He kissed her. She kissed him back like only Gretchen could—giving him her all. When she drew away, her smile was soft.

"Do you know what I think is the best word in the dictionary?" she asked.

He took another sip of her sweet lips. "Love."

"That's a good one, but it's not my favorite. My favorite word is *home*."

Her declaration caused his heart to tighten, and he pulled her close and brushed his lips over her forehead. "You're home now, baby."

She nodded. "I know. I've come to realize that

a home isn't a structure made of wood, stone, and walls. Or even a fairytale castle on a hill. My mama always used to say that 'Home is where your heart is.' But I think it should be the other way around. 'Heart is where your home is.'" She drew back and placed her hand on his chest right above his heart. "My home is right here."

He didn't think he could love her any more, but he realized he'd been wrong. Looking into her beloved green eyes, he placed his hand over her heart.

"Then I guess we're both home."

## THE END

*Turn the page for a special*
SNEAK PEEK
*of the next Kingman Ranch novel.*

# SNEAK PEEK!
## *Charming a Fairytale Cowboy,*
Coming August 26, 2022!

❈

THERE WAS RICH.

And the there was filthy rich.

As Shane Ransom stepped out of his beat-up Dodge pickup, he couldn't help staring in open-mouthed awe at the huge stone castle with its turrets that stretched up into the dark Texas night sky.

So this was Buckinghorse Palace. When his brother had first mentioned the name the townsfolk had given the Kingmans' house, Shane had laughed his ass off. But he wasn't laughing now. This *was* a palace fit for a king. After growing up in a rusty trailer with one bathroom, Shane couldn't help feeling envious. But one day, he'd have his own castle on a hill. Come hell or high water.

"Hey, Reverend Ransom!"

Shane turned to find a chubby teenager standing there grinning from ear to ear, the moonlight glinting off his braces. The greeting didn't surprise Shane. Folks confused him for his twin brother,

Chance, all the time. But he *was* surprised by the kid's ten-gallon hat and gun and holster.

Noting his confusion, the kid whipped out the plastic gun and fired a few caps into the air. "It's all part of my costume. I'm Hoss from the old TV show, *Bonanza*. My grandma loves Hoss."

Shane liked the kid on the spot. Not only because he was a *Bonanza* fan, but also because he had wanted to make his grandma happy.

"Grandmas should be catered to for the short time they are on this earth," he said. Something Shane wished he'd learned sooner.

The kid slipped the toy gun back in his holster. "If you give me your keys, I'll park your truck. The Kingmans don't want people parking in front." Shane tossed him his keys and the kid gave him a valet stub. As he hopped behind the wheel, the teenager shook his head. "I thought a preacher would drive something fancier."

Shane quoted a bible scripture his grandma had always quoted whenever he asked for something they couldn't afford. "'For we brought nothing into this world, and it is certain we can carry nothing out.'" When the kid looked even more confusion, Shane laughed. "You're right. It's a piece of shit truck."

The kid's mouth dropped open in shock and Shane should've told him he wasn't a preacher. But while Chance was a saint, Shane had always been a little bit of a devil. And pretending to be his brother was one of his favorite things to do. So he only winked before he headed toward the castle.

The huge oak front doors with their intricately engraved Ks were fit for a castle. Shane rang the doorbell, then stood back to wait. When several minutes passed, he figured the doorbell couldn't be heard over the loud country music and laughter coming from the house so he opened the door and stepped inside.

The inside was as impressive as the outside. The foyer had polished marble floors and a high ceiling with a domed skylight. From the skylight hung a glistening chandelier with gold prancing horses intermingled with the dangling crystals. The foyer was filled with people all dressed in western costumes.

There was no way Shane was going to find his brother in this crowd.

He pulled out his cellphone and texted Chance. I'm here. Where are you?

A second later, his phone pinged with a reply.

Forgot to set the church alarm. Had to run back to town. Do NOT go inside until I get back. Bubbles appeared on the screen before another text came in. I mean it, Shane. I don't want you causing any more confusion than you already have.

Shane smiled as he texted back.

You know I live to confuse people. He could almost see his brother gritting his teeth. Shane figured he'd screwed with Chance enough and quickly texted again. I'll be waiting for you out front.

He pocketed his phone and went to leave when a woman's voice stopped him.

"Reverend Ransom!"

He turned to find a short, stocky woman in what looked like an Annie Oakley costume hurrying toward him. In the brown wig, it took him a moment to recognize Kitty Carson. When he did, he mentally groaned. Chance had wanted him to stay under the town's radar until he could officially introduce him. Unfortunately, Kitty *was* the town's radar. She not only delivered mail to the town of Cursed, Texas. She also delivered all its gossip.

He pinned on a smile. "Well, hey, Ms. Carson. How are you?"

She put a hand on her hip and flashed a bucktoothed smile. "I'm Annie tonight. I wanted to be Miss Kitty from *Gunsmoke*, but my boobs overflowed the costume." She gave him the onceover. "Casey from Yellowstone? Although that's not an old western. And isn't his character a little violent for a preacher?"

It looked like he was going to have to come clean. "I'm not really a preacher. I'm Chance's—"

Before he could say brother, her eyes narrowed on something over his shoulder. "The gall of that woman. I'm glad you're taking over for Reverend Floyd. The man refused to do anything about Hester Malone. But I know you're not the type of man who will let a witch continue to practice her witchcraft in our Godly town."

Shane turned to see a tall, gray haired woman in a gypsy costume talking with a big man dressed like John Wayne.

Kitty shook her tower of red curls in disgust.

"A gypsy. What does a gypsy have to do with old westerns? She even brought a crystal ball. Now if that isn't the sign of a witch, I don't know what is. I think you should march right over there and let her know that her ungodly costume is not welcome at this church fundraiser."

He started to explain that he wasn't his brother when her eyes widened. "See what I mean? She's trying to curse me with her evil eye right now." Before he could even process the craziness, Kitty ducked into the large room off the foyer.

Once she was gone, Shane glanced back at Hester Malone. He had to admit she had a penetrating stare. It seemed to be burning straight through him. Just like it had the first time he'd shown up in Cursed. Hester had been the only one who had seen through his farce.

Shane hadn't meant any harm by doing the twin switch. He'd just wanted to make sure Chance was happy. After losing his wife, Chance had gone through a rough patch and quit his job pastoring at the church in Dallas. Shane had taken it upon himself to look for a new position for his brother. When he'd seen the town's name in an online ad for a pastor, he'd been intrigued.

So Shane had come to Cursed and pretended to be his brother to see if it would be a good fit. The friendly people and warm welcomed he'd received had convinced him Cursed was the perfect place for Chance to heal. He'd gone back to Dallas and talked his brother into applying for the job. Chance hadn't known anything about the twin swap until he'd come to town. When he found out, he hadn't been happy.

And he'd be even less happy if Shane caused more trouble.

Shane tipped his hat at Hester before he slipped out the door.

With some time to kill before Chance got there, he decided to look around. To the right of the castle was an elaborate garden with all kinds of trees, plants, and flowers and a quaint cottage that looked like it came right out of a storybook. Granny Ran would've loved it. She might have lived in a rusted old trailer, but she had grown the most beautiful flowers and biggest vegetables at her trailer park.

The garden path was lined with bronze statues of the championship horses raised on the ranch. At the end of the path, Shane came to stone steps. He followed them down to a hedge maze. He'd always loved puzzles. As he was walking through the maze, he noticed the sound of trickling water. He followed it to a break in the hedge. When he stepped through, the sight that greeted him took him by surprised.

It was a secret garden complete with a lush lawn, vibrant spring flowers, a beautiful tile fountain with cascading water . . . and a garden fairy.

Although the woman who sat on the edge of the fountain with her feet dangling in the moonlit pool of water didn't look like a fairy as much as a siren. Her red salon-girl dress was hiked up to her knees, showing off shapely legs. Her dark curls fell around her shoulders, playing peek-a-boo with the soft swells of her breasts above the low-cut neckline.

As he watched from the shadow of the hedge, she tossed something into the fountain and paused for a moment. Then she reached for the bottle of champagne sitting on the ledge next to her and took a deep swig. She set the bottle down and released a long sigh.

"Some ball, Karl. I didn't even get asked to dance once."

Shane glanced around for a man, but all he saw was a mean-looking goat munching on some flowers.

The woman splashed her feet in the water. "I mean is it too much to ask for a man who has enough guts to ask me to dance?"

Shane moved out of the shadow of the hedge and took off his cowboy hat. "Would you like to dance?"

The woman startled and placed a hand on her chest. "Jesus!" He was about to apologize for scaring her when her eyes widened. "You." He thought she had mistaken him for his brother . . . until she continued. "You're the cowboy I kissed at Nasty Jack's bar."

Now he was the one surprised. He stepped closer and studied her features in the moonlight. "You're the pool-playing cowgirl? The one who took all my money?"

She pulled her feet out of the fountain and stood. "I didn't take it. You bet it."

"After you conned me into it."

She sent him the sassy smile that had haunted his dreams for the last few months. "All's unfair in love and pool."

Shane laughed. Suddenly, coming to the Kingman Ranch so his brother could introduce him to the townsfolk of Cursed wasn't such a waste of time. Shane remembered the night at the only bar in town. He remembered it well. It wasn't because a girl had bested him at pool. It was because after besting him, she had followed him outside and kissed him like no woman had ever kissed him before. He'd wanted more, but the old guy who ran the bar had run him off with a gun. Still, Shane had thought about that night often and wondered what would've happened if the old man hadn't shown up.

Now he had a chance to find out. If her smile was any indication, she was as happy to see him as he was to see her.

"So what you doing here?" she asked.

"I was supposed to meet my brother at the Cowboy Ball, but he's running late. So I thought I'd take a look around the infamous Kingman Ranch."

"And what do you think?"

"It's more over-the-top than I thought it would be. I mean who builds a castle on a Texas ranch?"

Her eyes narrowed. "Maybe a man who can afford to."

So she was just like the rest of the town. The townsfolk of Cursed thought the Kingmans could do no wrong. He understood. From what his brother had told him, the Kingman Ranch employed half the town and helped support the other half.

He held up his hand. "I didn't mean any offense. A castle just seems a little odd for a ranch."

She relaxed and reached out to pet the goat that now didn't look mean as much as love struck. It looked up at the woman with big, adoring eyes. "I guess it is pretty odd. And wasteful. The money could've been spent on better things."

"So what are you doing out here when there's a ball going on in a castle?" He hesitated. "I don't believe for a second that no one asked you to dance."

She turned the goat toward the break in the hedge and patted its butt. "Go on now, Karl. You shouldn't be in here eating all the flowers." When the goat was gone, she looked back at Shane. "It's true. The only ones who asked me to dance were my brothers."

He studied her features in the moonlight. Her hair was as black as a moonless night. Her nose had a cute little tilt on the end. She had the kind of mouth that easily smiled. And expressive eyes that couldn't lie. Right now, they held a sadness that touched his heart.

"Then you have a town of dumbasses." He set his cowboy hat on the fountain ledge and held out his hand. "May I have this dance, miss?"

She lifted her eyebrows. "With no music?"

He cocked his head. "There's music. Don't you hear it? The crickets sound a little off-key, but the trickling water is as pitch perfect as any country ballad."

There was a moment when he thought she'd decline. Then she took his hand. She wasn't a small woman. Even shoeless, she was only a half a head shorter than he was in his boots. But she seemed to fit perfectly in his arms.

She smelled good. Not like perfume or lotions and hair products. Her scent was simple. Clean soap and something earthy. If the tan on her arms was any indication, she spent a lot of time outdoors—at something that took physical strength. Her arms had definition. He started to ask her what she did for a living, but then stopped himself. The thought of keeping his mystery girl a mystery was titillating.

He waltzed her around the fountain. The fifth time around, he spun her under his arm before lowering her into a dip. When he set her back on her feet, she swayed and he placed a hand on her waist to steady her.

"You okay?"

She nodded. "The spinning just made me a little dizzy."

"Are you sure it's not the champagne?"

"I didn't drink that much. It was almost empty by the time I got here."

He grinned. "So you're only slightly drunk."

"More like slightly buzzed. But not enough that I couldn't lay you out if you tried something I didn't like."

His gaze locked with hers. At the bar, her cowboy hat had shadowed her eyes so he hadn't been able to tell their color. Now he knew they were a startling blue that reflected the moonlight like twin mountain lakes. In them, he saw the exact need that ate at him.

A need for something more.

Shane lowered his head. "In that case, I'll only do things you like."

Preorder
**CHARMING A FAIRYTALE COWBOY**
from Amazon!
*https://tinyurl.com/yc6xebt2*

# Other Titles by Katie Lane

Be sure to check out all of Katie Lane's novels!
*www.katielanebooks.com*

### Kingman Ranch Series
*Charming a Texas Beast*
*Charming a Knight in Cowboy Boots*
*Charming a Big Bad Texan*
*Charming a Fairytale Cowboy (Coming August 2022)*

### Bad Boy Ranch Series:
*Taming a Texas Bad Boy*
*Taming a Texas Rebel*
*Taming a Texas Charmer*
*Taming a Texas Heartbreaker*
*Taming a Texas Devil*
*Taming a Texas Rascal*
*Taming a Texas Tease*
*Taming a Texas Christmas Cowboy*

### Brides of Bliss Texas Series:
*Spring Texas Bride*
*Summer Texas Bride*
*Autumn Texas Bride*
*Christmas Texas Bride*

### Tender Heart Texas Series:
*Falling for Tender Heart*

*Falling Head Over Boots*
*Falling for a Texas Hellion*
*Falling for a Cowboy's Smile*
*Falling for a Christmas Cowboy*

### Deep in the Heart of Texas Series:
*Going Cowboy Crazy*
*Make Mine a Bad Boy*
*Catch Me a Cowboy*
*Trouble in Texas*
*Flirting with Texas*
*A Match Made in Texas*
*The Last Cowboy in Texas*
*My Big Fat Texas Wedding*

### Overnight Billionaires Series:
*A Billionaire Between the Sheets*
*A Billionaire After Dark*
*Waking up with a Billionaire*

### Hunk for the Holidays Series:
*Hunk for the Holidays*
*Ring in the Holidays*
*Unwrapped*

# About the Author

KATIE LANE IS a firm believer that love conquers all and laughter is the best medicine. Which is why you'll find plenty of humor and happily-ever-afters in her contemporary and western contemporary romance novels. A USA Today Bestselling Author, she has written numerous series, including *Deep in the Heart of Texas, Hunk for the Holidays, Overnight Billionaires, Tender Heart Texas, The Brides of Bliss Texas, Bad Boy Ranch,* and *Kingman Ranch.* Katie lives in Albuquerque, New Mexico, and when she's not writing, she enjoys reading, eating chocolate (dark, please), and snuggling with her high school sweetheart and Cairn Terrier, Roo.

For more on her writing life or just to chat, check out Katie here:
Facebook *www.facebook.com/katielaneauthor*
Instagram *www.instagram.com/katielanebooks*

And for information on upcoming releases and great giveaways, be sure to sign up for her mailing list at *www.katielanebooks.com*!